FOREWORD

CERTAIN THINGS IN LIFE ARE TAKEN FOR GRANTED, especially those which are constantly with us. For example, the sound of a siren does not concern us as it perhaps once did. Some of us may rush to the window to see if it is a police car, ambulance or fire truck and wonder what happened or feel somewhat frightened when driving and a siren is suddenly behind us. But we are always reassured—whatever it may be—will be taken care of by the brave men and women in the service industry.

We have taken them for granted far too long.

The tragedy of the World Trade Center in New York gave us a deeper realization of the bravery of these men and women and the sacrifices they constantly make.

This novel brings you into the first years of Garth Winters' life as a firefighter. As you step into his world, you will be given a glimpse of the structure of a firefighter's life more than fifty years ago in a major Canadian city.

You will be apprised of how the firefighters had to counterbalance the anxiety they felt after struggling in vain to save a life. Humour became their only cure for post-traumatic situations. It came in the form of pranks constantly played on one another. You will find the pranks chronicled on these pages outrageous and unbelievable but they are, nonetheless, true.

You will follow the life of Garth Winters, age 25, as he adjusts to his new career and meets the woman of his dreams.

You will also witness Garth's ultimate act of forgiveness.

Technically, much remains the same in today's fire halls, however, years ago the psyche of the firefighter was very different.

This novel is dedicated to all the brave men and women: firefighters, first responders, police and armed forces, and anyone who daily puts their life on the line to help others.

The authors would like to thank the following people for their contribution towards the completion of this novel:

Trevor and Giselle Cradduck; Georgina Gropp;Pamela Waechter: Bert and Linda Hadley.

Val would especially like to thank the many firefighters he worked with over the years whose association was the birth of this story.

TESTIMONIAL

Marie Rickwood's most recent novel, *Behind the Smoke*, successfully portrays the life of a firefighter in a Canadian Prairie City. It reveals how initial antagonisms between characters changes when embroiled in a life threatening situation. The beauty of this book are the self-contained chapters allowing one to either read them in sequence or come back later to pick up another episode in the life of Firefighter Garth Winters. It is indeed, an interesting read.

CHAPTER

1

EXHAUSTED FROM A LONG, STRESS-FILLED DAY, Garth Winters trudged down the sidewalk like a tired soldier and clambered up the twenty steps to the door of his apartment. He opened it, stepped in and allowed the heavy door to swing shut with a bang. Its noise resonated to every corner of his small, one-bedroom apartment.

It had been a long, drawn-out day—and a disappointing one. When trying to close the only prospective sale of the entire week at the used-car lot, his commission had slipped through his fingers like loonies most often do at a casino.

Why do people come shopping for a car when they know damn well they cannot get credit? he thought. *Cockroaches!*

Garth glanced toward the doorway and noticed a large, brown envelope scrunched up in the mail slot. He removed his tie, hung it on the hook by the door, and then snatched up the envelope. He didn't open it immediately. Instead, he just walked into the kitchen, where the smell of stale coffee lingered, and tossed the envelope and keys amongst the crumbs on the table.

Garth took a deep breath and released an exasperated sigh. He was perspiring heavily.

"Phew! I need a shower and a cold beer!" he said.

His parched throat took precedence. Two long strides closed the distance between himself and the refrigerator. He cracked open a beer and took a drink, and then sat down at the kitchen table, his attention focused on the envelope. Garth turned it over and checked its origin: Personnel Office, City Hall, 620 Blake Street, Papillon, Saskatchewan. That could only mean one thing—he was finally getting a response to his application for the firefighter's position which had been advertised.

The fire chief had informed him at the interview that he would hear back within a few weeks. A few months was more like it. Hell, he'd almost given up hope.

At twenty-five years old, Garth Winters was considered a tough man by any tough-man-standard. But, beneath all that brawn, his hand trembled slightly when he opened the envelope. He was anxious. Perhaps it was because his last two jobs had been nothing but the pits.

Garth had spent four years driving an eighteen-wheeler up the treacherous Alaskan Highway, putting his life in his hands while white-knuckling the steering wheel. Then one Saturday morning while in his hotel room in Juneau, he noticed an ad for a Used Car Salesman in Papillon, Saskatchewan, a city almost the size of Regina, not too far from the farm where he'd grown up. The city is named after its first settler; a French biologist who had moved to the area at the turn of the century from Quebec. He had owned one of the largest collections of butterfly specimens in the world. When the city was formed it was deemed appropriate to name it Papillon—French for butterfly.

Garth had decided selling cars would be, if nothing else, safer than driving a truck. However, it wasn't long before he realized he'd much rather slip off the icy road into a ditch than screw the little man on his trade-in. That little piece of truth always ran amuck with his conscience.

He'd been promoted to manager after only four months. His surprise and delight quickly dissipated when he realized his only competitors—an ex-con and a pool hustler—could not pass the rules for being bonded.

There were a number of other unsavoury characters connected with the used car business. One in particular was the clerk from the finance company. He was a short, obese man, who insisted on doing the interview in the applicant's home. He'd purposely put the fear of God in them—should they ever miss a payment—by walking around their house and marking down the serial numbers of all their major appliances.

Last week had been a rare exception. A beautiful, tall brunette had come into the lot. After a quick tour she'd made her choice. Garth could still hear the financial representative's twangy voice questioning her as he gazed out the office window at the vehicle she'd chosen to purchase—a lime green Pontiac that'd been taking up space on the lot for over a year.

"Hmm, good choice, my dear. Hmm, where exactly is your source of payments?" When trying to act casual, his singsong tone was always there.

She shifted in her chair, fluttered her long eyelashes, and gave him a slow smile. "I'm sitting on them," she replied just above a whisper.

The man remained unmoved and stoic, almost as if he had expected that answer. Garth was astonished. Obviously the man had processed prostitutes in the past. He half expected him to tip her over and look for the serial number.

Garth would have no trouble whatsoever in leaving the grotty business of selling used cars. The more he thought about, the more disgusted he'd become. He hoped the letter in his hand would be good news.

It was.

The letter was dated September 1st, 1965. He was told to report to the Training Centre of the Papillon Fire Department at 8:00 AM on the 15th of February, 1966. Furthermore, he was requested to make an appointment with the city's doctor so the attached medical form could be completed.

Relief ran through his body! "Yes, at last, a job with substance!" he exclaimed. "A future – hooray!"

All his life, Garth had admired firefighters. At a very young age, he was mesmerized by the big red trucks barrelling down the road to put a fire out. It seemed surreal that now he was actually going to become one. He was excited and ready to meet the challenges this new job would inevitably place before him.

CHAPTER

2

FEBRUARY, THE MIDDLE OF WINTER IN THE CANADIAN Prairies, spreads a white blanket across its expanse connecting with the cerulean sky while sunshine casts a thousand diamonds on its surface. But on occasion, blustering snow blows in with drifts piling high across roadways. It is then, with the wind factor, the temperature sinks far below freezing, temporarily putting an end to winter's bliss.

When Garth Winters reported to the training centre, it was all of that and more. In fact, it was the worst weather ever recorded for the Canadian province of Saskatchewan at this time of year.

Garth was unfamiliar with the fire-fighting business; he had never even entered a fire station, nor did he know anyone who was a firefighter. He didn't know what to expect, yet he had no reservations entering this new terrain with the knowledge that he would adapt quickly.

Upon reaching the training centre, he encountered a number of men with weather-flushed cheeks and anxious faces parking their cars. As he'd suspected, they were his fellow trainees.

As they approached the entrance, the door opened wide and they were greeted by a tall, middle-aged man dressed in an officer's uniform. From his crested, navy hat with the gold band above the peak, to his brass-buttoned tunic fitting neatly over matching trousers, this was a man who obviously wore his uniform with pride.

The seriousness he attached to his assignment showed on his stern countenance when he announced in a loud voice, "Welcome, gentlemen. I assume you all are here for training."

He quickly glanced around the men with his eyes coming to rest on the tallest, Garth Winters. *He's a strong one,* he thought.

"My name is Captain Simco. Come on in."

They followed the captain into a large, warm classroom, where the distinct aroma of coffee filled the air. The snow that had clung to their clothes was already starting to thaw. Two officers sat at desks: one was labelled 'Chief of Training', and the other, 'Training Officer'. In front of their desks stood a flip chart, and to the side of it was a table with a number of pamphlets of information. Positioned in front of the officers were desks and chairs for the trainees. In the corner of the room was a fridge and table with a pot of fresh coffee and cups. One wall contained a large bulletin board, while the other held a large window, which delivered the merest suggestion of light from the bleak outside world.

"Please," said the captain, "put your lunch in that fridge and then take a seat. There should be twelve of you." He counted them under his breath as they sat down and then called out each name from a list he held in his hand.

"I see you're all here. I trust you all have brought your medical report. I'll collect them now."

The austerity of his countenance softened as he gathered them and marked something on his list.

"So you want to be firefighters, do you? Time will tell whether you make the grade." The remark was meant to be a warning: it wasn't going to be a cakewalk.

The captain cleared his throat and continued, "We are going to be training for six weeks. Half the time will be in this classroom. The other half will be on the training grounds. You will learn how to operate apparatus used at a fire and at a medical aid call. As First Responders, you will be given extensive First Aid Training and learn how to establish triage at an accident scene. For those who do not know what that means, it's applying medical priorities. But your training won't stop there; you will learn something new every time you climb on a pump and head out to a call.

Pump and aerial are the firefighter's terms for the truck; aerial is the one with the ladder on top.

"Halfway through your training, you will jump out of the window of a three-storey building. You will practice on the first- and second-storey, and then jump out the third. There will be men at the bottom with a net marked with a big red circle to catch you. At some stage in your firefighting career, you may be trapped and need to escape, and you may also assist victims jump as well."

Some of the trainees were seen to be visibly gulping. It did not go unnoticed by the captain, and prompted him to add: "Perhaps some of you might just change your mind about being a firefighter by the time we're through.

You will also be trained to enter a burning building to search for possible victims that are alive or dead. You will be taught how to extinguish fires. Naturally, our main objective is to save lives."

He looked at each face and was pleased that he had their utmost attention.

"Now, I would like you to meet our Chief of Training, Chief Gillespie."

A short, rotund man in uniform came forward from his desk. Garth looked him over and instantly thought his appearance did not fit his title. In contrast to Captain Simco, his uniform—due to his girth—did not fit neatly. It was identical in every way with exception of his white shirt and extra stripes of service on the sleeves of his tunic. And although he was trying to assume an attitude of authority, Garth could see a twinkle in his eye.

His voice was raspy.

"I would like to take this time to wish you all good luck with your training. Becoming a firefighter is a noble profession. You must wear your uniform with pride and with the knowledge that you are helping your fellow man. There were three hundred and eighty-three applicants for this job. We chose only twelve. So you men can consider yourselves elite."

The men turned and looked at each nodding and raising their eyebrows. Without question, his statement made them feel important.

"There are three things, however, that are absolutely prohibited in the fire department, which could result in instant dismissal. You must not discuss religion, race, or politics."

He placed his attention on a man in the front, grinned and asked, "What nationality are you?"

"Italian, Sir," he replied.

"I suppose you are a Catholic, socialistic son of bitch!" stated the chief, breaking forth in laughter.

Soon the men were laughing with him. Garth, once he recovered from shock, laughed the loudest.

One thing I know, he's telling us this won't be a stuffy place to work, he thought.

The chief continued: "Well, it's nice to see you all have a sense of humour. Trust me, it is needed in this life-saving business. I will be giving a few lectures over the course of your training and look forward to working with you all."

His smile reached everyone in the room. He was beginning to speak again when he was interrupted by the excited voice of Captain Simco, who was standing by the window gazing outside into the distance. "There must be a fire downtown," he said. "I can see dark smoke visible through the snow!"

The jovial mood in the room quickly became sombre.

"Yes, there is," said the chief. "I was informed early this morning when it broke out. It's a three-alarm at the peanut warehouse. I'd have thought they'd have it out by now."

The words had no sooner left his mouth when an ear-jangling ring came from his office next door. The men jumped in their seats as the chief scurried across the room. They could all hear his conversation.

"Yes, yes, I understand. I have twelve recruits who have just arrived for training. I'll send them right away."

The men looked at each other with stunned faces.

They're sending us somewhere already, thought Garth.

The chief hurried back into the classroom and spoke quietly to the captain, then returned to his office.

"Gentlemen," said Simco. "We have an emergency. There's a little job we must do before we begin our classes. There is a large fire at the peanut warehouse. The hoses used in that fire have to be rolled and returned to Station No. 1. I have to issue your bunker gear and give you a quick lesson on how to roll a hose *properly.*"

He emphasized 'properly' making Garth think there must be a science to it. He was amused.

"Grab your coats and follow me."

They followed the instructor to the storeroom where they were given their bunker gear: long water-proof coats and overalls, high rubber boots, a helmet and two pairs of gloves each. All the gear was bright yellow.

When handing out the gloves, the instructor said, "It's important they be kept wet at all times if you don't want your hands to freeze," he said. "Over there on that wall you'll see hooks with your names above where you can hang your gear when we come back."

They followed him onto the apparatus floor. It housed an older pump and aerial, which was used for training purposes, and many other pieces of equipment needed for specific applications in fighting a fire or responding to an accident call.

At one end was a rack with three rows of hose of different dimensions. Though, it was primarily fifty-foot lengths. The instructor threw one out to unravel on the floor.

"Make sure it is flat and begin rolling with the male coupling end first to protect the threads and roll as tightly as possible. Do you have any questions?"

He paused, and without any response, he added, "I didn't think there would be, it's quite basic."

After a twenty-minute lunch break, the trainees were herded outside and climbed a ladder into the back of a one-ton dump truck.

Simco removed the ladder then jumped in beside the driver and shouted, "OK, lets go."

The twelve recruits—now wearing helmets with liners covering their ears and with shoulders hunched as they braced the weather-huddled together in the back of the dump truck on a mission to roll hoses. The blizzard blew bitterly around them, flapping their collars and the slanting snow bit hard into their faces. A faint smell of smoke was in the air.

None of the recruits had expected to be attending a fire scene on their first day of training, and none had expected to be riding in the cold open-air in the back of a truck during a hard blizzard. But Garth still couldn't squelch the excitement he was feeling.

"This is nothing but bullshit!" snarled recruit Marvin Hawks, his voice shaking and his teeth chattering. "If this is the kind of respect we get, I'm n-n-not sure I want this Goddamn job." He wiped his nose on his sleeve.

You're going to have to endure much worse than this, you sniffling little weasel. That is if you pass the training, Garth thought.

"Did you think working as a firefighter was going to be a walk in the park? Give your head a shake," quipped Garth.

The logic of his remark drew loud laughter from the others, which continued for several minutes, keeping company with the wailing wind as though it was relieving the tension. But it also drew a menacing glare from Hawks.

"I didn't expect we'd be treated like cattle," he retorted.

Garth didn't continue the debate, he'd made his point.

Short of a bus, a truck is the quickest way to move twelve men to the scene, he thought.

From the dark look he'd received from Hawks, he knew he had made an enemy.

As they drove up to Station No. 1, one block from the burning peanut warehouse, acrid odour filled the air and heavy black smoke, mixed with the blowing snow, swirled around them.

When they arrived at the ramp, they were met by Captain Andrew, who was expecting them. He introduced himself and gave them explicit instructions.

"When you get on site, *remember*: I am your officer and the *only* officer at this incident. Do not take directions or orders from anyone else. If another officer tries to give you an order to enter the burning building, do not go under any circumstance. Tell him you are a new recruit and that Captain Andrew is your officer. It doesn't matter if he's a captain, lieutenant, or even a chief. Tell him you take orders only from Captain Andrew, and if they have an issue with that, tell them to come and see me. Don't do anything but work with the hoses. Do you understand me?"

"Yes, Sir!" they harmonized in response.

"I will be sending a truck over to the site for the rolled hoses and appliances to be brought back here to Station No. 1. You'll have to manually carry the frozen ones. It's not a long walk."

He nodded to Garth and continued: "I want you to take the lead." Garth smiled, pleased to be given the responsibility. He nodded in agreement.

Hawks looked over at Garth. *Who does that bastard think he is?* If looks could have killed, Garth would've been deader than a fly on a windshield.

Bracing the elements, they walked the block to the peanut warehouse. Twelve men in yellow bunker suits made quite a sight. The acrid smell intensified as they drew near the fire.

The building was totally engulfed! What a vision it was. Bright red flames shooting up in the air through the white of falling snow interspersed with heavy, black smoke.

Six pumps, two aerials with many hand lines were on site to extinguish the fire in this three-storey building. The intensity of the heat turned the spray to steam before it reached the fire. In fact, it proved to be a futile attempt.

It wasn't extinguished after all as thought earlier by Training Chief, Gillespie.

Several policemen were holding back a crowd of onlookers jostling for a better look. Blackened gunny sacks filled with scorched peanuts lay everywhere and while there was a burnt odour in the air, there was also the intense, appetizing smell of roasting peanuts.

The chief-in-charge called a halt to his men.

"Too late fellas!" he shouted. "We're just going to let it burn. We're lucky this building is surrounded by a parking lot and there's no buildings close by. A fresh crew is coming on to keep an eye on the site and will continue to spray. Thanks for your efforts."

The bedraggled firefighters, on the job since early morning, walked slowly from the site in their blackened and ice-covered bunker suits.

Captain Andrew shouted to his trainees, "OK, guys, let's get the job done."

Ready for their instructions, the trainees gathered around Garth. Hawks stood a few feet back. His reluctance to cooperate was evident.

What is wrong with that man? Garth wondered

Garth found a partially frozen hose to roll, which proved challenging. The others followed suit and then eventually piled them into the back of the truck. They were met with a greater challenge, however, which was to finish the job. Lying on the ground next to the aerial were three, one hundred-foot lengths of hose covered with ice, which were twisted in all directions like three large anacondas.

Garth arranged the men in groups of four, each of them ten feet apart carrying one length. At his count of three, the men hoisted the heavy frozen, twisted line on their shoulders for the walk back to Station No. 1.

Garth saw Hawks following the others. He looked over in his direction and heard him say, "Who the hell does that tall son of a bitch think he is?"

His comment was ignored by the other men.

As they marched forward, one of the men—who'd had military training-boomed in a loud voice, "Left, right, left, right!" Soon all the trainees were shouting with him and keeping in step. This drew hoots, hollers and laughter from the other firefighters—tired as they were —leaving the scene. They appreciated the new recruits were mixing a little humour into a major catastrophe.

***

The next morning, the six-week training period continued with a full agenda—half in the classroom and half on-site. Over that period, they were taught and given, on-site instructions: how to administer stabilization to all types of injuries and rescues, and how to treat and analyze all types of disasters and fires.

They were also taught to water down all adjacent build-ings, trees and shrubbery, and the handling of tall aerial ladders and safe operation of the fire engines in heavy traffic. The most difficult task was quickly evaluating the situation and deciding the best method to use when rescuing people from a burning building.

Garth enjoyed all of the training and he achieved high marks on the weekly exams. He made friends with all but one of the fellow trainees who were all from different backgrounds. However, friendship did not happen with Hawks. He carried a grudge from that first day on the truck and had been envious by Garth being handed a lead role. Garth had expected he would've walked off the job by now, yet surprisingly he remained.

The fire house training occurred on the last day. It was a simulated house with sliding walls filled with choking smoke. Here, they learned to enter a smoke-filled building, look for victims alive or dead, and rescue them from the building.

The SCBA (self-contained breathing apparatus) was strapped to Garth's back and his mask securely placed on his mouth. He took a deep breath to assure its effectiveness.

Simco had assigned three trainees to bring out a manikin dummy. Much to Garth's chagrin, Hawks was one of them.

They entered the fire house together. They were challenged to find and check each bedroom, find and remove a manikin through the back door and accomplish this all within three minutes. The task would have been easier indeed, without the encumbrance of a dummy, but neither was an easy task in a pitch black, smoke-filled house with acidity that could kill.

Feeling his way along the walls and then sliding his fingers across the main floor, Garth found the first bedroom. There was no dummy there; the room was empty. Searching frantically, he found the staircase, and started to make his way up, when he heard someone on the staircase, directly behind him. Garth turned around just in time to see a shadowy figure quickly turn and descend. He took a deep breath to continue up, but the face mask vacuumed tight to his face. He reached for the control valve at his waist but he had no air, so he turned and hurried down the stairs, stumbling and falling on the last step, he managed to get up.

Where the hell's the door? I have to get out of here?

Panic stricken, he quickly felt his way along the walls. His heart was beating hard and fast against his ribcage and he thought he was about to die.

By a miracle, a very small shaft of light indicated the doorway. He hurried to it and busted out, ripped off his mask, took a deep breath and slunk down against the door panting. He knew he'd been sabotaged!

***

Chief Gillespie straightened the few papers on his desk and gazed out towards the empty classroom—empty for the first time in six weeks.

Despite the odour of lingering smoke from the hours spent on a fire site, it was an exciting time when the men were training. He knew—shaped from the gruelling six weeks—there would be firefighters ready to meet the challenge of their job. That made him happy.

He enjoyed his lectures in the classroom when he could lighten the air with some humour. This day, however, was a day he would sooner have behind him. Captain Simco and the new recruit, Garth Winters, were due in his office any moment.

Garth Winters was a tall, young man with vivid-blue eyes and black curly hair, who stood out from the rest of the trainees. His demeanour was one of confidence and capability. He found it hard to believe that the dreadful event had occurred only yesterday in front of the smoke house.

Simco arrived first and went to his desk at the head of the classroom and put down the sheaf of exam papers. Garth was right behind him.

"Rest your arses and spare the feet," Chief Gillespie announced jovially, motioning to chairs.

Both men sat down in front of his desk.

"This is the first time in ages that I've had to have a meeting such as this," said the chief. "We have some talking to do." His switch from joviality to seriousness was palpable.

Garth shifted in his chair. *Damn it anyway! I've really blown it this time. Just when I've found a job I really like.* He waited pensively, prepared for the worst.

"In all my years in the fire department, never have I had to deal with an altercation like what happened yesterday," said the chief. "Marvin Hawks has told me his side of the story. Now, Garth, I want to hear yours. I want you to tell me exactly what happened."

Garth shifted in his chair and cleared his throat.

"I was climbing the tower stairs when I felt someone bump me from behind. Immediately, I lost my air. I turned and could see someone hurrying down the stairs. It was Hawks."

"Just a minute, how can you be sure it was Hawks, it's pitch black in there? And how do you know it wasn't just a malfunction?"

"I saw part of his name on the back of his bunker suit. So it had to be him."

"Then what happened?" asked the chief.

"I thought I was a goner but finally found the door and got out. I sank down on the porch grateful for air. It was the scariest moment of my life."

Garth paused.

"And?" asked the chief.

"It took me a few moments to get my wind back when Hawks came up the sidewalk and shouted at me. *'Why are you down on your ass, Winters? Did you think this was going to be a walk in the park? By the way did you run out of air?'*

He laughed like it was one big joke."

Garth looked at the chief with eyes that spelled sincerity.

"It was then that I lost it. I got to my feet, stepped down to the sidewalk and," he paused, "and drove him."

"You damn near broke his jaw is what you did! Do you realize you might have killed him? He was out cold and had to be revived."

Garth met the chief's unwavering gaze.

"He damn near killed me. I was lucky to have found the door!"

"We would have dealt with it and the captain would have come in for you. Physical violence isn't the answer," replied the chief. But he was thinking, *I would have done the same damn thing if it had been me.* "There are rules in the fire department about physical violence. I have to give you three-month probation. It will be added to your usual six-month probationary period as a new recruit."

Relief washed over Garth's face. He looked at Captain Simco who was trying to conceal a smile.

Once outside the building, Simco turned to Garth.

"If it makes you feel any better, and remember you did not hear this from me, I'm going to recommend Hawks be given *six* additional months. He is being interviewed again later today. I bet he will claim it was a practical joke."

"Some joke!" replied Garth. "There was nothing practical about it whatsoever!"

"Oh, by the way," said the captain with a faint smile on his face. "You finished your training at the top of your class. Congratulations! On Monday morning, you are to report to Fire Station No. 5. There you will start your career as a firefighter. I wish you lots of luck, buddy. And for your information, Hawks will be at Station No. 3. Encountering him again won't be often, if at all."

They shook hands.

CHAPTER

3

AFTER A LONG, BITTER, PRAIRIE WINTER, THE SPRING thaw came early. Melting snow splashed down off rooftops, little rivulets gurgled down the drains and the snow, once a pure white, had become murky, brown slush.

Garth remembered the blizzard on his first day of training and by contrast much preferred the thaw. He was excited about starting a new job, especially now at twenty-five years old, he was more than ready to settle down in a new career and positive future.

His parents believed in training their son well. From his mother came his integrity and from his father, strong work ethics. His father gave him the chance to do many things on the farm. Garth loved riding the tractor over the back section-pulling a plough, disc or harrow. He learned the importance of tending the soil if one wanted a good harvest.

But it was reaping the fruits of their labour—the combining—that he loved most of all.

Being the eldest of four, he relished the many responsibilities given to him. From his father, he'd learned the mechanics of farm equipment; how to deal with livestock and butcher when meat was needed, and how to fall trees with a chainsaw to make firewood for the long, cold winter months. But most of all he had learned how to work. He had strengthened his body by playing hockey throughout his high school years and had excelled in the sport, yet it just wasn't in the cards to make it his career.

It was Saturday morning—the day after training—when Garth decided to take a look at his new Fire Station, No. 5. He was met by a friendly firefighter on duty in the Watch Box; the post where the firefighter meets the public and opens the overhead door when a pump has to leave.

He was shown where to check his shift schedule and was told the station was manned twenty-four hours a day, non-stop. When they saw Garth's first day was on Monday morning, he was shown how to place his gear next to the vehicle for expedience sake. He didn't explore beyond the area of the Watch Box, but returned home eager for Monday morning—ready to be a firefighter.

When Monday arrived, Garth went to work early. He was welcomed by Captain Savage and shown around the station. He was surprised to see the station was much like a cozy home, all on one level. There were, however, two storeys to the building. The second storey was where Chief Hadley, who headed all the fire districts in Papillon, had his offices and staff. There was a private side entrance to his quarters, and from his office window he could look down on the deck and yard of the fire station below.

Chief Hadley was referred to by his subordinates as the Head Honcho. He had given the final interview to each firefighter (including Garth) in Papillon and for that reason—and perhaps for his dignified presence—he commanded respect from everyone.

The hub of the station was the large kitchen centred by a table with ten chairs, where several men who had come off nightshift had just shared a joke. They were all laughing and barely nodded when Captain Savage said, "This is Garth Winters, our new rookie."

Across the room, a six-burner gas stove held a gurgling coffee pot. Through the kitchen an entertainment room could be seen. It contained a television where three firefighters were watching a sports channel and two others were having a heated discussion at a pool table nearby as to whether the called shot was a clean one. There were several lounging chairs and against one wall was a large bookcase containing well-used literature regarding up-dated firefighting and first responder procedures and equipment. The dorms consisted of a row of single cots and adjacent lockers.

"There's your bunk, and there's your locker with your name on it," said Captain Savage. "You can put your lunch in your locker, or in the fridge in the kitchen. Just make sure your name is on it, because if you don't someone will eat it up—firefighters are a hungry lot.

"We take turns cooking meals and all pitch in a few bucks to buy the food, and then believe me, we take our chances. There are a few who consider themselves excellent cooks, which I would say is debatable. And then there are some who are pretty damn good at it. Actually there's one guy who's a better cook than my wife, but I'd never tell her that." He released a low chuckle.

Garth laughed. "Gotcha, thanks."

"Over there is the main bathroom. There are four sinks, four urinals and showers. The officers and District Chief have their facilities in separate quarters."

They walked on, entering a doorway leading to a large open area. Garth's eyes widened at the sight of the big red apparatuses. He recalled how as a child how he would become excited at the sight of a fire truck racing down the road with its siren wailing. They appeared so much bigger when in close proximity.

"Here is all of our apparatus: the aerial, the pump, the rescue, and the District Chief's vehicle. As you can see they all face a gigantic overhead, roll-up door ready to depart. It is fully staffed in less than a minute, even if you firefighters have been in bed. You learn how to cut the mustard here and scamper like hell."

Captain Savage gestured toward a room close to the overhead doors. "That over there is the Watch Box. It is manned twenty-four hours a day to service the public. Night shifts are fourteen hours and day shifts are ten. The firefighter on duty in the Watch Box has to operate the doors, greet the public when they visit the station, and any new firefighters that are coming on force.

"Most importantly, when a call comes in from communications—the separate branch that disperses the necessary equipment and personnel to any given emergency—he marks down the address, gives it to the driver and raises the door, and they're off.

"Now, let's go check your shift."

"I've done that," said Garth. "I was here on Saturday and was shown the shift roster by the man in the Watch Box. I know I'm on rescue. I have my gear in place."

"Great," said the captain. "You're all set to go and you're just in time for roll call. Oh, I almost forgot to tell you, firefighters have time on their hands so they do all the cleaning. The new rookie on the job is always in charge of cleaning the bathrooms. There's a closet in the hall with all the supplies you'll need. When you come on shift that will be the first thing you'll do. There are a total of four bathrooms in the building, which includes that big one I just showed you. One of the guys will show you where they all are."

The captain gave Garth a discerning look, as if expecting some negative reaction, but got none. After shovelling manure on a farm, it remained unlikely that Garth would be daunted by cleaning a few toilets. .

As they started across the room, a voice came over the PA System.

"Station No. 5, Station No. 5, there's a body in the river at 87th Street!"

Garth stopped short and looked at the captain. "Holy crap, I think that's for me."

The captain nodded and said, "I'll be partnered with you."

They raced over to the rescue vehicle, quickly donned their bunker suits, and stepped inside. They were joined by Bradley, who was the driver. The Watch Box attendant came running with a piece of paper with the address, and then the door went up and they were off with the siren wailing. This emergency procedure had taken less than a minute to perform, and for Garth, his new job as a trained firefighter had begun.

The sound of the siren parted the busy morning traffic from each side of the road, leaving an unobstructed trail.

The fire engine pulled up to the river bank at 87th Street and the firefighters quickly ran through the slushy snow to the shore. They could hear the rushing sound of water running fast with chunks of ice adrift. The air was cool and fresh on their faces. In the distance, the sound of a city coming to life could be heard.

"Where's the body?" questioned Garth as his eyes searched the crusted water.

"It's gotta be here somewhere," said the captain. Bradley stood guardedly two feet back.

"There it is!" shouted Garth with excitement.

Before anyone could respond, he was rushing into the icy water toward a snagged bush. Beneath the bush and barely visible in the water was a bloated body of a woman, all shades of black, purple and blue. Her face and body looked like they had been blown up like a balloon.

As the body bobbed up and down and finally surfaced, Garth had his first sniff of a rotting corpse. He squelched a sickening urge to say goodbye to his breakfast and could not stop heaving as he reached into the water to drag the body to shore. He grasped an arm, and to his absolute horror, it detached from the body. He could see slimy, brown fluid running out of the end of it and mixing into the water as he held it. Garth almost toppled backwards but managed to regain his position against the strong current.

So intent on his mission, and with a sequence of events occurring so rapidly, he did not hear the captain shouting in a loud, angry voice.

"No, Garth! No! Garth Winters, don't touch the body! Don't touch it! DO YOU HEAR ME!?" His loud voice carried down the river.

The captain's voice brought him back to his senses, so Garth finally turned and slowly made his way back through the icy water, and climbed the snowy bank to the shore.

"Sorry about that, Captain. I thought someone had to be saved."

"Hell no, no one can survive those waters more than a few minutes. You went in before I could stop you. The ID police unit is expected any moment. They'll go in and take pictures for identification. Then we'll go in and scoop the body up on a stretcher and give it to the ambulance men."

"I see. What do they do with the body?"

"They take it to the morgue, of course."

Sirens could be heard coming closer. Within minutes, the I D police unit and the ambulance pulled up simultaneously.

"The body is engaged down there," said the captain, pointing towards the dark, rushing water.

"I'll have to go into the water to take pictures," said the officer. "Oh hell, I have no boots." He looked around at the three men.

"You can borrow mine," said Garth. "Our feet look about the same size."

"Great, I won't take long."

Garth placed his coat on the ground to stand on and then handed his boots over to the policeman. Once pictures had been taken and the firefighters had laid the body on a stretcher, they handed it over to the ambulance driver who then drove off to the morgue.

"Well done," said the captain nodding at the two men.

No one would have ever believed that after only twenty minutes into his new job, Garth would have walked into an icy river, pulled the arm off a corpse and loaned his boots to a policeman.

Hearing the compliment from the captain, Garth raised his shoulders and feigned a smile, which was a habit he'd adopted since childhood.

This episode will live with me forever, he thought.

CHAPTER

4

AFTER TWO WEEKS OF TEASING, GARTH WAS RELIEVED that the nickname of 'One Arm Winters' had finally come to an end. He had had more than enough of the jibes that had come his way, but thankfully, his patience and refusal to retaliate had paid off.

The spring thaw and intermittent freezing created an ice hazard on the highways and many calls came in for medical aid. Fires were also on the upswing. After the long winter, the inhabitants of Papillon had become careless in tending to their fireplaces and wood stoves.

Garth's adjustment to his new occupation had been faster than average. He learned that fires don't wait for anyone, and the saving of human lives from smoke inhalation and heat was based entirely upon the speed at which firefighter comes to their rescue. Fire consumes oxygen from the air in minutes and can take a life very quickly. Firefighters learn the importance of being quick and pride themselves in clearing the fire station in less than a minute after a call comes in—even on nightshift.

Garth took pride that he was always the first on the pump. He arranged his bunker suit in such a way that he could virtually jump into it almost before the alarm stopped ringing. He had developed a safeguard for such a time when he would be called to an accident or fire scene and his adrenalin was bubbling over—a personal motto: *"Be quick and fix."* This adage calmed him and allowed him to look past the horror and concentrate on the task ahead. Nonetheless, the firefighting job had changed his countenance and thereby his demeanour.

One morning, after three months on the job, Garth stood shaving. He stopped and gazed at himself in the mirror and was unnerved by the face of a stranger. Had the role of a fire-fighter, witnessing highway carnage, dead bodies and being reduced to sorrow, taken its toll on him.

And, as the days passed, Garth also learned of the unspoken safety guard, a protection of sanity throughout the fire station understood by everyone, which came in the form of humour. Pranks and tricks on each other were often a great antidote, which helped to ease the stress.

Ex-boxer District Chief Watson, sat quietly in the background tending to paperwork and making sure the full complement of the firefighters within his district was always met. Seniority transferred him into his position, and while he kept a low profile for the most part, his quiet deliberation got the job done.

Captain Carmichael, on the other hand, who had replaced Savage, ran the station with aplomb and humour.

"Well if it isn't Garth Winters," said the captain. "How are you doing man? You've been on the job now for about three months, right?"

"Yep, it's been that long."

"We've had the busiest spring ever. You pretty much know what fire fighting's all about by now. How do you like it so far?"

"Actually, I quite enjoy it. There's definitely more to it than I would have imagined."

Garth studied the face of the captain. He saw a man with half a grin on his face and devilry in his eyes. So many stories about him had circulated amongst the guys; how he owned a hairdressing shop downtown and how his first wife caught him in a compromising situation in the backroom with one of the junior hairdressers.

"I can tell you like your work," said the captain. "You are always the first one on the pump. One of these days I'm going to beat you there."

"I wouldn't bet the farm on that," laughed Garth as he headed over to the pool table while the captain went to take a shower.

Garth got one shot in and the captain had just finished undressing and was about to step into the shower when the bell rang. The voice was shrill.

"Station 5, Station 3, fire at the Rona Apartments on 71st Street. Man trapped."

The men flew to their bunker gear and to the pump. The captain was first on the pump just ahead of Garth.

How did he ever manage that? There goes the farm!, he thought.

"Let's go, let's go!" the captain shouted.

The door was raised, and the man on watch ran over with the address and they were off.

When they arrived at the scene, the fire had progressed rapidly. A large crowd had gathered outside, and cheered as the rescue services arrived, and were equally animated as the firefighters went about their duties.

The apartment building, which was in the north end of town, had become a landmark and they were going to do their best to save it.

Inhabitants huddled together in the parking lot. Some were crying, others holding their faces.

Captain Jones, from Station No. 3, was the first to arrive at the scene and had believed the building to be totally evacuated. But alas, he was wrong. Up on the third floor, a man's face could be seen at the window; like the call said, there was a man trapped. It was a shock to everyone, especially Captain Jones. He shouted for a ladder. It was quickly raised up to the window and Captain Carmichael ran ahead of everyone and clambered up the ladder faster than a Mexican gecko across a concrete wall.

As he climbed up the ladder, a gust of wind whipped his long coat up, raising it up to reveal to all below on the ground that he was devoid of trousers and even underwear. Despite the shock, laughter ensued, and one firefighter shouted to a group of ladies standing nearby.

"Come and have a peek at the humming bird sitting on its nest."

Captain Carmichael heard it but didn't care a whit. His job was to save the man—and that was exactly what he was about to do. Carefully, he guided the man down, step by step. It was just in the nick of time, as the roof caved in shortly after.

Garth, who had been working at the other end of the building, wasn't there to see it but he heard all about it later at the station.

Now I know why he was first to the pump. He ran from the shower and put on his coat and jumped into his boots naked as a jay bird!

He chuckled to himself. And for a few moments juggled the thought of whether the nakedness was competition to beat him to the pump or dedication. He thought about it for a few seconds, recalling the urgency in his voice when he had shouted, "Let's go, let's go!" Then he knew it was pure dedication.

The captain's teasing at the station took on monumental proportions, day after day, lasting way longer than the one-arm saga. He was getting tired of all the nicknames, razzing and innuendos. Frankly, it was getting on his nerves.

The captain knew he had to do something to put a stop to it. Something that would really shock them. Something that would stick in their memories for a very long time. *But what can I do?* he wondered. He thought about it for days; when he went to bed at night, in the middle of the night, and when he awoke in the morning. Each idea he had, he'd end up thinking, *Nah, that's too predictable, not shocking enough. It has to be something that will really jar them.*

Finally, he felt he had an idea that would work but he needed the help of another firefighter. But who? That was the question.

I know, I'll get that new guy, Garth Winters. He looks like someone who would cooperate with me. Besides, he won't say no to his boss.

"I need your help with something, Winters," said the captain. "Are you on shift tomorrow morning? I believe you are."

"Yes, I am. What can I do for you?"

They sat in a far corner of the station. Garth listened intently as the captain explained what he wanted him to do.

"Tomorrow morning when we're all sitting around the table having coffee, I will nod to you when I leave the room; that will be your signal. After five minutes, and you must clock it, I want you to leave the table. Ask the guys if anyone has seen a watch around. Tell them you've lost yours and that you're going to look for it. Then you come into the dorm. I'll be there."

The captain paused with a silly grin on his face.

"What exactly are you expecting me to do and why?" queried Garth, feeling a bit suspicious knowing this captain's reputation.

"I'll be pretending to be sick and you will summon the men to come and help. That's all."

"But why?" questioned Garth.

"As you know, I have been the object of their teasing for quite some time and I want to put a stop to it. Do you blame me?"

"Not at all," replied Garth. "I know how they taunted me unmercifully and called me, 'One Arm Winters' after the body in the river episode. I'll do what you ask."

The next day, however, a dark shroud hung over the station like a thunder cloud. The men sat glumly sipping their coffee, eyes blurry and heads downcast, as they reflected on the previous day when they were called to battle a fire at a nursing home in the north end of town. Despite the efforts of all the firefighters, many of the elderly residents and young caregivers perished.

The men had come in for a coffee, exhausted and sad from their futile efforts. They were bereft of dialogue and it would take days for the firefighters to rid their minds of the disaster. No one was watching television or playing pool.

The captain stood up at the table. His prank couldn't have come at a better time. He raised his eyebrows and nodded at Garth to let him know the plan was in motion.

What on earth is this man up to? Garth wondered.

Garth kept glancing at the clock on the stove and when five minutes passed, he stood up and said, "Has anyone seen my watch? I'm going to search around for it."

He was gone for a few minutes then rushed back to the table with brows knitted in a frown and feigning rapid breathing.

"Come quick!" he panted. "Something is wrong with the captain! I heard loud moaning coming from his dorm."

Garth's performance was worthy of an academy award.

The men, who were instantly on their feet, knocked back their chairs and then rushed down the hall as fast as their tired feet would carry them. When they entered the captain's dorm, they found him huddled in a far corner facing the wall whimpering like a lost nanny goat.

They hurried towards him with anxious questions and panic on their faces:

"What's the matter, Captain?"

"Should we call an ambulance?"

"Do you have a stomach ache?"

"Where do you hurt?"

When the captain finally turned around, all that could be heard was a cacophony of gasps, a discordant mixture of sounds escaping from their mouths. Their faces were whiter than fresh snowfall.

Hanging out of the captain's fly was a long, brown, swollen member, the size of a milk bottle.

"The old doze has come back again," whimpered the captain.

"H-h-holy shit!" gasped Garth. He'd never seen anything like it in all his life.

No, this can't be the hoax he was planning, it can't be! This is for real! The poor devil!

Seeing the effect he was having, the captain decided to call a halt to his prank. He reached into his pocket and pulled what appeared to be a string and rolled his eyes back as he released the disgusting appendage from the front of his pants. It landed on the floor. Plunk!

He threw his head back and laughed.

"Fooled you, fooled you! You've been teasing me for days about me bare arse, and now I've given you the other side to tease me about!"

He laughed again so loudly it could be heard down the hall, through the television and pool table room, through the kitchen, and finally clear across the equipment room where the apparatus were stored and all the way into the ears of the man in the Watch Box.

The firefighters walked out one by one, some grinning, others chuckling and some still looking aghast.

"Where the hell is our chief when we need him?" said Barry Taylor, one firefighter who refused to see the humour.

"No doubt he's out doing his rounds," replied Garth. "He normally does them at this time of the day."

"Well, I'm going to tell him all about this atrocity. I've never been so nauseated! What was that thing hanging out of his pants?"

Barry held a handkerchief next to his mouth.

"Having lived on a farm, I would hunch it was the genitalia of a dead horse. He must have picked it up from the slaughter house at the other end of town on his way to work," replied Garth.

"The crazy bugger! My wife will never believe this!" Barry put his handkerchief back in his pocket and walked away mumbling.

Garth was thinking. *If I'd known he was going to go to this extreme, I wouldn't have been party to it but how do you turn your boss down when you're the new kid on the block.*

But, as he thought about it further he realized the end result of the prank was two-fold. It would put a stop to the teasing, but more importantly, it would take the firefighters' minds off the recent disaster.

As Garth walked to the kitchen to get another cup of coffee, the alarm rang. This time there was a cat up a tree on Second Street.

CHAPTER

5

DISTRICT CHIEF WATSON MADE IT HIS BUSINESS TO GET TO know each firefighter under his supervision. A fair-minded man, he was always understanding. Although he was an amiable character, his men knew he wasn't one to be crossed. What they did not fully realize was that their district chief was constantly under the watchful eye and scrutiny of the head honcho upstairs, Chief Hadley, who had the power of Hercules when it came to the careers of the district chiefs under his command in Papillon.

Watson's thoughts turned to the new recruit, Garth Winters. Despite the fighting incident with Marvin Hawks when he was in training, he was showing a lot of promise. He'd read the incident report over carefully and couldn't help applaud Winters for his action; that kind of tough man, with some tempering of course, would make way for a great firefighter. Watson decided that, when the time arrived, he would strongly recommend that Winters be promoted to the rank of captain. But much could happen before then.

He thought about Captain Carmichael who, when hearing the call of a man trapped in a fire, had hurried partly clothed to try and save his life. A minute after the safe rescue, the roof had collapsed. While firemen accept saving lives as part of their jobs, Watson felt that he should congratulate Carmichael personally when he saw him again.

Suddenly, there was a loud knock on the door.

"Come in," he called out.

Barry Taylor walked through the door with a frown on his face and a purpose on his mind.

The chief looked at the firefighter who stood in front of his desk. He was a rather small man with sharp, aquiline features. He was a newcomer to his station, so he barely knew him. His only impression of him on the few occasions he'd seen him around the station was that he was reserved, quiet and bashful; the type of man that fades into the background.

I wonder what this visit is all about.

"What can I do for you, Mr., Mr., uh? I just cannot bring your name to mind."

"Taylor, Barry Taylor," he replied. "I'm on nightshift tonight but I've come in especially to discuss something very important with you. Something very private."

"Shoot," said the chief with raised eyebrows and a surprised tone.

"I was wondering, Chief, if you have someone to watch over the station for you? Keep you informed, so to speak. I know you are away from the station for long periods of time." He cast his eyes down humbly waiting for a reply.

The chief studied his face, trying to figure out where he was going with that question.

"I have a captain to do that. By the way, how long have you been a firefighter? Are you looking for a promotion before your time?"

"No, no, nothing like that," stammered Taylor. "I mean someone to be your private watchdog, to let you know if there has been something going on you'd want to know about that perhaps the captain wouldn't tell you."

"Oh, I get it. You want to be my little stoolie. My little snitch. My informer, so to speak."

The chief chuckled but he decided to play along to find out what prompted his proposition.

Taylor cleared his throat and began to look uneasy.

Why is he laughing? It isn't a laughing matter, thought Taylor. "Don't you want to know what's happening around here, Sir?"

"Of course, I do. What makes you think I don't?"

"Well," replied Taylor, "do you know what happened here last Friday morning for example?"

He was getting so brave.

"I know you are dying to tell me. So shoot."

"OK, then, this is what happened. Captain Carmichael pretended he was sick with what he called the old dose."

"The old dose?" queried the chief, who was doing his best to keep from laughing. He'd heard about some of this captain's antics but never about the old dose.

"Yeah, you'll never believe this. He had a dead horse's dink hanging out of his fly and made us all look at it. It made me so sick I almost vomited."

The chief put his head back and laughed uproariously. "He did what?" He laughed again. "Is that what you've come to tell me? Is that why you want to be my snitch?"

Without waiting for a response, he stood up quickly, knocking his stapler to the floor. His voice was loud and his words were clipped: "I don't have, and never will have a snitch. So take your sorry arse out of here. Do you understand me?"

Dumbfounded by the chief's response, Taylor nodded, turned on his heel with a face like a ripe tomato. He walked out swiftly.

The chief sat at his desk annoyed and amused at the same time. This prank of Carmichael's couldn't have come at a better time. The crew were down-trodden. They had just come through a fatal and most disastrous fire. They needed something to take their minds off the tragedy.

One thing he knew for certain, Taylor was one firefighter he would not endorse for promotion.

***

Garth sat quietly on the sofa reading the paper. He was on nightshift, and for the first time in a long while, things were relatively quiet at the station. Most of the men were in their bunks taking a much-needed reprieve, as the threat of a potential emergency call was always a probability.

He checked his watch: 11:00 PM. It was time to head off to bed, but he wasn't tired. After reading every syllable of the sports section, he put the paper on the end table, stood up and stretched. He remembered the novel, 'Never Cry Wolf', which was in his car, so he decided to go and get it, and then read for a while. Reading always made him sleepy.

As he walked across the lit parking lot, he noticed a shabby-dressed lady stumbling towards the station. She appeared to be intoxicated. She was staggering and the back of her brown coat was covered in dirt, and her hair was matted to her head.

"I need a place to sleep," she slurred. "I need a place to sleep. Can't anyone help a poor old lady find a bed?"

To his surprise, Taylor came out onto the steps. Garth saw him speaking softly to the lady but could not hear what he'd said. She stood there waiting. He shut the door and then returned a few minutes later and motioned for her to follow. Stumbling, she tailed him around the building to the outside staircase.

Taylor quickly glanced around but did not see Garth in the shadows, he then half-lifted, and half-pushed the lady up the staircase, opened the outside door and took her inside.

Garth stood for several minutes, pondering what he'd just witnessed and trying to make sense of it all. He couldn't.

Mighty strange piece of business! he thought.

He shrugged as if to dismiss the thought and then made his way back up to his room and went to bed, hopeful that he could read for a spell and then fall asleep without a call coming in. He reached up and turned off his light and fell asleep with his book on his chest.

It was 7:30 AM when head honcho, Chief Hadley, pulled into the parking lot. He was feeling on top of the world. Things were going great on the home front, and equally as good with the fire stations in Papillon. City Administrator, Don Symington, with whom he recently shared a lunch, complimented him once again on how well-organized his stations were and what excellent firefighters he was turning out.

Receiving compliments from his boss always raised his spirits. This day there was a new spring to his step as he walked across the parking lot of Station No. 5.

However, that morning when he walked into his office, he was immediately greeted with a strong odour of urine. Lying on his sofa was a filthy, drunken lady, who was snoring like a swine at the trough. He raised his hand over his mouth and then quickly left the room, running down the stairs towards District Chief Watson's office.

"What the hell has happened to the security of this place, Watson? I have an uninvited guest in my office. Would you believe a street lady is sleeping on my sofa?"

"A what? You've got to be kidding! How the hell did she get into your office?"

"That's what I'm asking you. You run this place!"

"It's that damn janitor! It has to be! My men are very conscientious about locking the doors. I've trained them to secure the building each night. It's a matter of routine. I'll talk to them and I'm certainly going to talk to the janitorial service."

He reached for the telephone but set it down when Hadley continued: "I don't care what you do! Just get to the bottom of it! I trust you to take care of this place but now you're giving me doubts. I want you to call Social Services to come immediately to get this, this woman out of my office. And then I want you to call the police, and, and, and also call Papillon Fumigators!"

A vein was popping on his neck.

"I'll do that right now," replied Watson, feeling like he was caught up in a wire trap.

As he was leaving the room, Hadley stopped and said, "Now I have to go downtown and pick out new office furniture. Have maintenance dispose of the old stuff."

That's a bit of a stretch, thought Watson. But it really didn't surprise him knowing how very particular the chief was when it came to cleanliness. He expected all the pumps in Papillon to be well-shone and the attire of the firefighters to be above reproach.

But, new furniture, really?!

Watson made the phone calls as Chief Hadley had requested and also dialled the janitorial service. He asked the manager to see him as soon as possible and told him it was extremely important.

Next he checked the shift roster on his desk to see who was on Watch Box duty. *Whoever it was has some questions to answer, and so do all the others that worked the nightshift,* he thought.

Frustrated and anxious, he left his office to round up all the firefighters. Breach of security was a serious matter.

A thousand thoughts were racing across his mind as he walked across the station. *What a shock Hadley must have had! How did that lady get in? Has to be the janitor! Has to be! Not one of the guys! Surely! Damn it anyway, this is all I need right now.*

He picked up the P.A. phone in the Watch Box and hollered into it, "Everybody on the floor now!"

Awakened by a shake on his shoulder by a co-worker, Garth jumped out of bed, causing his book to drop to the floor. Immediately, he dressed and hurried out to the television room, where every firefighter in the building was, including those who were just starting their shift, and those who were about to leave.

Watson stood in the centre of the room. The men had never seen him looking so upset. His face was red and his eyes were blazing. He spoke slowly and deliberately in a low monotone. "A terrible thing happened in this station last night and now my position is on the line. We had an intruder. Somehow or other, a door was left open, and when Chief Hadley came into work this morning, he discovered a bag lady had come in off the streets and was sleeping on his sofa in his office."

He no sooner got the words out when the men broke into laughter, which continued for several minutes.

"This is no laughing matter!" shouted Watson over the din. The tone of his voice calmed them down to a snicker. "When Chief Hadley arrived at work this morning, the side door to the building was unlocked, his office door was unlocked and his keys lay on his desk. He knew he'd put them on the rack inside the Watch Room and he knew he had locked all the doors when he left. Safety is a big issue with the chief and with me.

"I have the janitorial service on their way over now; they were working in this building last night. They have a lot of explaining to do.

"I know none of you men would place our building in jeopardy, or play some kind of sick joke on our chief or myself. I want you to know I'm certainly not blaming any one of you. However, I am asking that from now on, you men on nightshift remember to check all the locks on all outside entrances without fail, before you go to bed, just as you were trained to do. Have I made myself clear?" There was a bead of foam on the corner of his mouth.

Garth stole a surreptitious glance at Taylor who was standing at the back. He saw the muscles moving in his cheek like he was clamping and then releasing his jaw.

But why would he play a trick like that on the chief? And how did he get the keys? he wondered.

He has a lot of courage to pull that kind of prank on the chief. He must have had a grudge against someone. But it couldn't be the chief, he doesn't have much to do with him, if anything. Unless he was trying to get even with District Chief Watson for one reason or another by getting him in trouble with the Head Honcho. He must have had a reason to do this. Cockroach!

"I will be meeting with each one of you. I know some of you are just finishing your shift, but when you come back on, I would like to you to come to my office."

The men sat around the table having coffee. They were all still feeling the sting of urgency in Watson's words, while seeing humour at the very thought of what had happened.

Just when Garth thought he'd seen and heard it all since starting with the fire department, this happened. The fire hall was definitely not a dull place; one prank after the other. However, this last one definitely topped them all.

Garth stood up and said, "Well, I can see you guys are all enjoying it. From my viewpoint, we can play tricks on each other to ease the stress of this job, but never on our superiors, especially not the man at the top. He has a big responsibility to keep the stations in this city running smoothly. Just think about it for a moment. If someone broke into this station and damaged our pumps we'd be in one hell of a fix if an alarm came in. I don't blame him for being angry."

He directed his attention to Barry Taylor. "You were on shift last night. Did you hear or see anything amiss?"

"Nope, I didn't," replied Barry.

He quickly unlocked his eyes from Garth's penetrating stare placing no doubt in his mind that Garth knew something, he could feel it. And Garth was thinking, *If honesty was dynamite he wouldn't be able to blow his nose!*

Garth finished his coffee, washed his cup and put it in the cupboard. He looked out the window at a small cavalcade of vehicles in the driveway: a police car, a van with social services written on its side, another van, black in colour, with the inscription of Papillon Fumigation, Inc. printed in bright yellow. His thoughts were galloping.

Should I tell Chief Watson I saw Taylor bring the woman up the stairs to Hadley's quarters or should I say nothing?

He squeezed his mind to get his thoughts around his conundrum. Was there not a Social Service car in the parking lot? One benefit that might come out of this prank is that the woman might get help that would take her off the streets. He balanced that thought with the utter insubordination shown by Taylor. After chewing on it for a few moments, he made his decision.

Just then he saw a furniture truck pull up. Two men got out and were greeted by Chief Hadley before they began to unload the new office furniture.

Hmmm. There's more than one benefit coming out of the prank!

When leaving to go home, he glanced back towards the kitchen and saw Taylor staring at him. He looked worried indeed.

When Garth returned on his shift at 6:00 PM, he decided to go see Watson directly to get *his* interview over with. He knocked on Watson's door before trying to open it, however, it was locked, which was unusual. Just then Watson appeared and unlocked it so Garth could enter. He had been having an in-depth conversation with another firefighter and had locked the door.

"Come in, Garth. I'm just finishing up here."

He smiled and Chief Watson smiled back. The friendly rapport between them was mutual.

"I won't keep you long, just need to ask you a few questions about what happened last night. Chief Hadley has come down on me mighty hard. As I've said, I'm responsible for everything that happens around here. Did you by any chance hear anything last night out of the ordinary?"

"I was engrossed in a new novel and read most of the evening. The station was quiet. I never heard anything out of the ordinary, Sir."

He felt by adding *Sir*, it would lend more credence to his less than honest reply. It wasn't in fact what he'd heard but what he'd seen. However, this day he wasn't about to rat on anyone; it just went against his grain, so to speak.

"OK, I just needed to ask you. I still have more men to speak with. I'll get to the bottom of it, one way or the other."

Watson interviewed the other men on nightshift, and the staff of the janitorial company, who all claimed they had locked everything up as usual. He was bewildered.

Days passed and turned into weeks and the mystery remained. Meanwhile, Chief Hadley sat upstairs on his new chair at his new desk admiring all the other new furniture. He didn't feel guilty about buying it, as the old stuff was exactly that—old. And he had quite a substantial amount in his contingency fund in the budget. He didn't pursue the issue of the break-in any further.

And the culprit, Barry Taylor, left the fire department to take a job with—of all things—a used car dealership. Garth was happy to see the back of him walk out the door. The mystery of how he was able to obtain the key to Chief Hadley's office remained a mystery.

CHAPTER

6

GARTH TOOK HIS TRAINING MANUAL FROM HIS locker, sat on his bunk and studied the organizational chart.

He thought about Chief Hadley, the man at the helm in charge of all fire stations in the city of Papillon. He was a tall, fastidious man who carried himself with dignity. Chief Hadley had a winning smile for the public, but his geniality stopped at the door of the fire stations. From there on in, it was pure business. He held the reputation of being the most proficient and effectual of all fire chiefs in the history of Papillon.

Hadley was popular in other ways, too. During his frequent visits to City Hall, the ladies on the staff had often whispered to one another that the handsome fire chief was in the building. They would strain their necks to get a glimpse of him.

The next in line were deputy chiefs, who were trained to fill in, followed by district chiefs, such as Watson. They headed all the stations within their districts. Last in line but, no less important, were the captains. They worked in close proximity with the firefighters, especially the new recruits.

Garth realized from his eight months on the job, like most work places, there was a pecking order that was carefully followed. A firefighter's interaction was predominantly with the captains.

And now the flamboyant Captain Carmichael, the man who beat him to the pump, who had left his mark on Station No. 5, albeit repugnant, was transferred. A new captain was coming on board.

What would he be like? If he's anything like Carmichael, life will never be dull at Station No. 5.

For some strange reason, Garth's thoughts brought Hawks to mind and how he almost lost his life when his oxygen had been disconnected. He expected to encounter him at a three-alarm fire (a time when several stations battled the blaze). But he had not seen the cockroach since the day he'd laid him out cold on the sidewalk.

He touched the knuckles on his right hand recalling the punch that landed squarely on Hawks' chin. While he regretted the incident, he did not regret the punch, one iota.

He left the dorm, walked into the kitchen and poured a coffee from the infamous brewing pot. Some days the coffee was so strong, one could almost chew it, but today it appeared better and the aroma was enticing.

He took his cup into the television room and sat down on the sofa. He was joined by two colleagues who had just laid down their cues and crossed the room to join him.

"I hear we're getting a new captain," said Dave, a short, stocky man known as the 'Champ of the Pool Table'.

"Yeah," said his pool partner, Gerald. "Someone to replace Carmichael. His name is Sean O'Sullivan. I hear he's a real prankster and will put Carmichael to shame."

"That would take some doing," commented Garth, recalling the old dose incident.

"Well, let me tell you what I know about him. He's fearless, don't give a damn about nothing and will do anything on a bet," said Gerald.

"He's a damn good firefighter. One of the best, I'll give him that," stated Dave.

"He has to have some promotional qualities to be a captain. What do you mean by 'he'll do anything on a bet'," questioned Garth, anxious to find out all he could about the new captain before he arrived.

"Story has it," continued Gerald, "once when he was a little short on cash, he went around his station taking bets that he could stand out in front of the fire station for three minutes holding up his right leg with one hand on his head and the other waving to cars."

"That's no great feat," said Dave. "It's just a matter of keeping one's balance."

"I guess that's what the guys thought. He never got any takers so he upped the ante, which I reckon was his ploy all along." The smile on Gerald's face told Garth he was anxious to get down to the nitty-gritty of the story.

"How did he up the ante?" queried Garth. He released a slow chuckle not knowing what to expect.

"His bet turned into, not three minutes but five, in his altogether . . . the full Monty."

"You've got to be kidding! Do you mean to tell me he actually stood naked in front of the station for five minutes waving to cars as they drove by?" laughed Garth. "Naked?"

"Yes, it's a fact. Well, not quite, he had his shoes and socks on," said Gerald. "Everyone placed a wager and Sean O'Sullivan walked away with over two hundred dollars. He didn't have the rank of captain then."

"I'm surprised he didn't get arrested for indecency," stated Garth.

"If a city cop had driven by within those five minutes, he might have," said Gerald.

"Oh, and another thing I heard something about O'Sullivan that I know you'll get a kick out of," said Dave.

"I'm going to really know this new captain before he gets here," joked Garth.

Dave ignored Garth's statement and continued: "On his day off, O'Sullivan was driving around Papillon to garage sales and he found this life-size statue of a Dalmatian dog. It had a battery in the back of its head which, when turned on, would move its head from side-to-side like it was counting cars. Apparently, it was so life-like one would think it was the real thing, from a bit of distance of course.

"He brought it to his station and positioned it on the balcony overlooking the parking lot. He wanted to play a trick on the district chief. That morning the guys were all sitting in the coffee room when the district chief came in and joined them.

"'Did I see a dog on the balcony when I drove in this morning?' he asked.

"'Oh, that's Luke. I'm surprised you didn't see him before. He's always been around,' replied O'Sullivan.

"'I didn't see him, nor did I hear him.'

"'You didn't see him because he sleeps a lot and you didn't hear him because Dalmatians don't bark.'

"'I see, I see,' said the district chief. 'It's quite a big dog, must cost a pretty penny to keep him fed.'

"'It's not very expensive because we all take turns buying the dog food. It's your turn tomorrow.'

"'I guess I don't have any choice in the matter. What kind should I buy?"

"'A small bag of dry dog food will be fine.'"

Dave began to chuckle and was anxious to finish the story. Garth's ears had perked and Gerald couldn't have been more attentive.

"The next day the guys at the table were all anxiously waiting for the chief to arrive. They kept looking out the window, when finally, they saw his car pull into the parking lot. He got out of his car and opened his trunk, and then took out a large bag of dog food and hoisted it up onto his shoulder.

"'Holy crap, he's bought fifty pounds of the stuff,' said one of the men.

"All of the guys at the table laughed. They had noticed him looking up at the balcony when he drove in. O'Sullivan had turned the statue on and the dog's head was counting cars again, so damn life-like.

"The chief came into the kitchen puffing and let the big bag fall to the floor by his chair. Ker plunk! He grabbed a coffee and sat down at the table looking mighty proud he was doing something wonderful for the canine world.

"He didn't seem to notice, the guys at the table were snickering. I guess he thought they'd just shared some kind of joke before he got there.

"He looked at O'Sullivan and asked, 'What am I to do with this now?'

"'Just take some out of the bag and dump it into the dish on the balcony.' He handed him a bucket. 'He's fed every morning and is mighty hungry right now. If dogs could talk, he'll be giving you a big thank you.'

"O'Sullivan had to cough to camouflage a chuckle rising up in his throat.

"'Better do it now.'

"The chief got up from the table, opened the bag, filled the bucket and headed upstairs.

"As soon as he had left the room, the guys broke out in laughter. All of them were waiting for him to return, which he did, of course. He stormed into the room with bucket in hand and shouted, 'I'm going to get you for this, you crazy bugger!'"

The men sitting around the table in the kitchen at Station No. 5, heard the laughter coming from the television room and wondered what was so funny.

***

Captain O'Sullivan didn't walk into Station No. 1—he strutted in like a he-man on a boardwalk. He planned his arrival to coincide with departure of one shift and the arrival of another. The bigger the audience the better. His men had to know who was leading them, and the sooner the better. He shook hands with the men that were coming off their shift and heading home, and then went into the kitchen area where the next shift was sitting around the table, having a coffee and shooting the breeze.

Sean O'Sullivan was a tall, well-built man. His head was bald since he had had it shaved for a bet. He had a space between his two front gold-filled teeth that on occasion made a little whistle when he spoke. Having served for a short time in the Navy, he had an ugly red scar that travelled down his left cheek; a cruel reminder of the attack he received in a foreign port. The scar represented his ego, considering it a sign of being macho. He had a short temper, which often placed him in altercations in bars all over town.

Today, he stood before the table with his chest puffed out and a lollipop clutched at the corner of his smiling mouth between his air-conditioned teeth.

He greeted the men in a deep voice. "I'm your new captain and my name is Sean O'Sullivan. Couldn't get any more Irish than that. You can call me Sully but never late for dinner. Tell me, are you fellas putting all the fires out?"

"Yup," was the harmonized reply echoing around the table.

"Damn well better be. Now, starting at the left, I'd like you all to state your name and how long you've been with the force. I want to know who the hell I'm leading. Who're the wise guys and who're the green horns, and whose arse I need to kick."

At the head of the table in an all-imposing stance, O'Sullivan shook hands with each man making some of them wince a bit from his grip. Garth was the last one to introduce himself and when he shook his hand, O'Sullivan said, "I see you have a good grip and I understand you also pack a pretty mean wallop."

Garth smiled and then shrugged his shoulders nonchalantly. *I suppose all the people in the city connected with firefighters are privy to that little piece of scandalous history.*

"I want you all to check the shift roster because I have made a few changes. I will be partnering up with each of you over a course of time. Tomorrow is your lucky day, Garth, as you and I will be working together. In the meantime, I will wallop any one of your arses at the pool table before I go to the back deck to get a tan; the bet's ten bucks . . . any takers?"

He gazed at the men one by one until finally, three of them accepted the challenge, however, three games later the captain was thirty dollars richer.

Garth arrived at work early the next day, eager to be on a call with the infamous Captain Sean O'Sullivan. He didn't have to wait long. Within a half-hour a call came in that a three-storey apartment building with a business on the ground floor was filling with smoke.

A strong tug of wind could be felt on the pump as they blazed down the road with the siren wailing. They arrived ahead of the other two stations to respond, which placed O'Sullivan in charge at the scene.

The middle-aged residents on the top floor initiated the alarm. There was a slight, blue haze of smoke in their pristine apartment and a strong odour of something burning. However, they were unable to locate the source, which frightened them.

Under O'Sullivan's careful guidance, both he and Garth performed a systematic search of the entire building. They started with the furnace room and then the office area, and all other parts of the basement. They checked the closets and other areas of the building, but were unable to find anything untoward. When they completed their search, the haze and odour had dissipated. Baffled, but realizing there was nothing more they could do, they left the scene.

Captain O'Sullivan felt thwarted by the perplexity and was quiet for the first time since arriving back at the station. Garth had been impressed by O'Sullivan's tenacity and thoroughness during the search and knew he didn't like to be stumped.

As they walked through the door of the station, the alarm was ringing. The tenants that had reported smoke in their apartment, were reportedly angry that the firemen had been unable to locate it while they had been there, and were less than hospitable when they returned to the scene.

"What's the matter with you guys? And you call yourselves firefighters, and you can't even find the fire! Just look at all this smoke! I'm going to report you to the city!"

The irate tenants were on the verge of panic. Garth and his captain began the search all over again. They could see some wisps of smoke coming out of the electrical receptacles in the walls then it stopped altogether. This time there was an odour of burning plastic.

Such a strange bit of business! thought Garth.

They made a thorough search of the building, but to no avail. O'Sullivan did his best in consoling the occupants, though they left the pump in the driveway next to the security truck as a precautionary measure, and then returned to the station by car.

"I cannot figure this out," said O'Sullivan. "It appears to be electrical but goes away before we can isolate the source. This is a son of a bitch if there ever was one!

Just what I need to wreck my reputation!"

The captain raised his eyebrows when Garth commented, "Sure puts a hole in 'where there's smoke, there's fire.'" His remark was ludicrous and he knew it so added: "Where there's smoke there *will* eventually be a fire."

"That's exactly what I fear," replied the captain.

When they arrived at the station, Garth said, "I'm going to go back in my car and drive around by the building. I won't be long, but in any case, if I hear the siren, I will join you on site."

Garth had a hunch. The apartment was a stucco building therefore had a wire mesh beneath the stucco.

Is it possible some electrical wire was contacting this metal? he thought.

When Garth returned, he parked his car and studied the hydro and telephone lines connected to the building. He got out of his car and examined the stucco. There was nothing amiss.

The power lines swayed gently in the breeze until a gust of wind came up and slapped a slack line against the top floor of the building. A spark flew, followed by another and another, which bounced off the stucco. When the wind died down, he looked up and could see a sizeable patch where the stucco had eroded. The construction mesh was exposed.

Garth heard the distinct sound of the siren and hurried to meet the captain in the yard. "I think I have the answer for you, Sir," he stated excitedly.

He took the captain around to the back where the sparking occurred.

"That must be it!" declared O'Sullivan equally excited. "We can take a better look out the window in the apartment. Let's go inside."

They hurried back to the top floor apartment. By this time, the irate tenants were packing their suitcases to leave.

"We're not staying in this damn place a minute longer," the tenant said.

The captain ignored him and walked through to the bedroom and opened the window. Sure enough, to the right below the eavestrough, there was some exposed mesh where the stucco had been rubbed off by the swinging wire, and the mesh was blackened indicating a scorching.

He walked back into the living room, picked up the phone and called communications. His tone bore an authoritative edge and sounded more like a command than a request.

"This is Captain O'Sullivan from Station No. 5. We have a serious electrical hazard at 1620 Omaha Street. Live wires are banging against the wire mesh on an outside wall of the building. Immediate attention is mandatory! We'll stay here until Saskatchewan Hydro arrives."

The firefighters realized the crisis would not be over until Saskatchewan Hydro arrived and corrected the situation.

The frightened tenants heard the call, looked at each other with relief, and stopped packing. The security man at the scene was informed, and in turn advised the owner.

On their way back to the station, O'Sullivan declared: "You saved my hide, Garth. I won't forget it! I owe you one. All I need is to fail on my first call when starting at a new station."

Garth smiled and shrugged his shoulders: "Think nothing of it," he said calmly.

CHAPTER

7

DISTRICT CHIEF WATSON SAT AT HIS DESK LOOKING over the weekly reports from the different stations within his jurisdiction that had gathered on the end of his desk. It always took a careful read to ascertain if any recommendations or changes were necessary. His motto was: "There's always room for improvement." He believed that an efficient firefighter was one who saved lives and put fires out." As he read the report, he made comments in the margins for future reference.

The electrical fire on Omaha Street did baffle him. The report by O'Sullivan stated they had meticulously checked both the inside and outside of the building. But why did it take the third call before they found the solution? This would definitely be a topic for discussion. Fortunately, they found the source. Had they not, a fire would have been disastrous on such a windy night. He thought about it for a few moments then wrote on the bottom of the report: *Make the inspection of power lines a mandatory part of routine checks.*

District Chief Watson was pleased with the thoroughness in which Captain O'Sullivan had written the report, and more than pleased that he'd found the source. He knew O'Sullivan was a proud, conscientious man and above reproach when it came to his job but a cantankerous rabble-rouser otherwise. His reputation had been following him around from station to station.

He planned to whip some of that mischief out of him at every opportunity he had. Actually, he'd quite enjoy the exercise.

***

Chief Hadley frequently looked out his upstairs office window. Most of his important decisions were wrought gazing clear to the horizon while jiggling the loose change in his pocket.

He always glanced down at the deck of the fire station below. He loved having his office in close proximity to one of his fire stations. It made him feel more in the loop, especially when he could witness them quickly departing in answer to a call; charging down the road in a big red fire engine with its siren howling. The sight of this always created an excitement in him and had done so since childhood. It was an excitement, he knew would never leave him. It was inevitable that he would have become the Head Honcho of all the fire stations in Papillon.

78

It was, however, one of these glances down to the deck below that he noticed the new captain with his shirt off laying prostrate on a lawn chair tanning himself. When he first saw him, he couldn't believe his eyes. Not only was he annoyed to see this, but he was also disgusted. Did he think the taxpayers were paying him to tan? And why wasn't Watson doing something about it? It was time for a talk.

The more he thought about it, the angrier he got and it was little wonder when he walked tall and erect into District Chief Watson's office, his voice cut through the air like a knife.

"What kind of signal are we giving the public? Are we telling them that their tax dollar is supporting a health spa? And how do they know who's in charge when they visit? Hell, he may as well be the janitor. The captain's insignia on his sleeve is a constant reminder of who's in charge, not only to his subordinates, but also to the public who frequent the station. I'm surprised you hadn't noticed and put a stop to it long ago. Are you blind, man? It's your job to put a halt to that damn nonsense. Do I make myself clear, Watson?"

He drew his hand across his mouth to wipe away the escaped spittle.

"Yes, Sir," replied Watson feeling bruised from the venom in his voice. But he knew the chief was right, he should have been aware. He should have known what was going on. Unfortunately he did not. He did not have a window to look out like the chief, besides, he was too busy. He had too much paperwork to do without looking out windows and spying on his staff.

With this scalding conversation fresh in his mind, he stormed off down the hall across the television room, to the kitchen area. As usual, the men were sitting around the table drinking coffee and conversing. He did not see O'Sullivan among them so he greeted the men and then made his way outside towards the deck.

Lying on his belly on a red lounge chair, and naked from the waist up, was the illustrious Captain O'Sullivan. The afternoon sun was beaming down on his already-tanned shoulders and glinting off the back of his bald head.

"Get your sorry arse up and stand to attention!" said Watson. His booming voice could be heard in the coffee room, which drew a hearty mix of raucous laughter around the table. O'Sullivan could hear the men laughing at his expense, and there was nothing he hated more than to be laughed at.

Watson's words were still floating in the air when O'Sullivan jumped to his feet. He did it with more agility than thought possible for a man his size.

"What do you think we're running around here, O'Sullivan, a British Columbia Health Spa? The chief could come down for an unexpected visit any time and there'd be hell to pay, damn it! Get your uniform on and be the captain you're supposed to be, or do I need to send you back to the training school? You know you must expose the insignia on your shirt sleeve at all times! Do I make myself clear or do I have to take further action?"

O'Sullivan instantly gazed up towards Chief Hadley's window. He saw a shadow move. *Ah ha! So that's where it's coming from. The Head Honcho instigated this reprimand.*

Not waiting for a response, Watson turned on his heel and returned to his office while O'Sullivan stood speechless, degraded and angry.

How dare anyone talk to me that way! How could I be so disrespected?

He couldn't face the men in the coffee room so slunk back to his dorm, planning his revenge. He knew he'd have to wait for the right opportunity, at just the right time, and at just the right moment. But he was going to get even, and get even he would!

Two days later, it was another bright, sunny day and Captain O'Sullivan could be seen by everyone tanning on the deck once again. The men saw him and thought nothing of it but Watson was livid. O'Sullivan was on his stomach, his big rump and huge frame spread leisurely out across the red lounge chair snoring up a storm. This time a towel was covering his left shoulder.

"O'Sullivan!" thundered Watson, his holler again reaching the ears of the men in the kitchen. "What did you not understand about our last conversation? I explicitly told you, you have to have your insignia showing on your arm and here you are again!" He gestured in the direction of the lounge. "This is a blatant case of insubordination. I've a good mind to ... to ..."

Once again, O'Sullivan was instantly on his feet like a jack-in-the-box before the chief could finish.

"You asked for an insignia, well what do you think this is?"

He exposed his right arm from under the towel and pointed at the exact replica of the firefighter's insignia, which was tattooed on his skin. He turned and exposed his left arm showing the same crest and then stood, grinning like the joker on a deck of cards.

"You are one crazy bugger! Put your shirt on and keep it on or I'll suspend you!"

What Watson didn't know was that O'Sullivan had paid an earlier visit to the Head Honcho upstairs to show him his tattoos. He had knocked on his door unabashed and opened the door before he'd heard him shout, "Come in." The chief had looked up from his desk in surprise. O'Sullivan spoke first: "The officer's insignia doesn't have to be a problem when I suntan."

Having delivered his statement, he stood staring at the chief with a smug look, successfully camouflaging a grin.

"Oh, and why would that be, pray tell?" the chief had asked, his voice coated with sarcasm.

O'Sullivan took off his shirt, flexed his muscles and displayed his tattoos of the insignia on both arms, which were still red from the needle. He stood there, his height superseding that of the chief's, grinning like he'd executed the trick of all tricks.

Chief Hadley had had the wind blown out of his sails, much to O'Sullivan's delight.

"If you know what's good for you, then get your miserable ass out of here and don't let me ever see you without your shirt on again, you juvenile delinquent!"

After O'Sullivan left, Chief Hadley asked himself, "Did that really just happen?" He couldn't get it out of his mind as he drove for an appointment to see the district chief on the other side of town.

That ended the tanning sessions for O'Sullivan but it didn't end his thoughts of revenge; it was hanging onto him like a bad cold. He was thinking of a way to get back at Chief Hadley. He knew if he was to get even with the chief, District Chief Watson would undoubtedly be adversely affected. To coin a phrase, "two birds with one stone".

***

Other than being a firefighter, Garth loved farming. On his days off from the station, he could be seen riding his horse on the land he had inherited from his father. The role a firefighter was demanding, yet he enjoyed the camaraderie with his colleagues and the prospect of saving lives. In spite of all that, he dreamed about the day when he would build his own home and find the right woman who would become his wife.

When it was time to return to the fire station, he would be renewed and ready for the tasks that lay ahead, never hedging, never flinching, and always ready to perform his duty to the full.

When he arrived at the station there was a buzz around the table about the new white Oldsmobile with its white-wall tires, and all its bells and whistles that Chief Watson had purchased.

"Why is it parked at the far end of the parking lot?" someone at the table asked.

Garth responded in a matter of fact tone: "I would think he's afraid of it being scratched. I cannot think of any other reason. Don't blame him though. I've had my vehicle marked up when parked and never did find out who it was. The cockroach got away with it."

"I noticed how he walks around it with his chest stuck out admiring it," said O'Sullivan. Sarcasm stuck to his comment like tar on the sidewalk.

"I hear those big cars gobble gas," said Garth. "And talking about gas, you won't believe this. At least *I* found it hard to believe. We were out on a call yesterday at a Chinese laundry on 5th Street.

"If ever there was a case of arson that sure was. From what we could tell, the fire started at the front office by the door where there was a small desk with papers on it. We put it out quickly so it never got past the office area. Later, when we were checking, we followed our noses down into the basement. It was an older building, a kind where the rafters are so low you have to duck. We saw at lease twenty plastic bags hanging from the rafters, and would you believe it, they were all filled with gasoline.

"If that fire had gotten away from us, can you just imagine the explosion? I think the whole street would have gone up in a blaze. I don't know how he thought he'd get away with it." Garth was shaking his head.

"I would have liked to see his insurance policy," said O'Sullivan refilling his cup at the stove. "Bet he never gets another."

When the shift came to an end the men walked across the car park to have a look at Watson's new car. Chief Watson was also heading home, so he greeted the men with a big, proud smile saying, "Straight home now, guys."

As he pulled out of the parking lot, the men shouted for his return. Having heard them, he stopped and got out of his car. "What's up?" he asked.

"Looks like there's a bit of oil on the ground beneath where you were parked," said one of the men.

"Can't be, this is a brand new car. It must have been there before I parked."

"Looks like fresh oil," said Garth leaning down and dabbing his finger on it. "I'd keep my eye on it if I were you, Chief."

Visibly upset, the chief turned on his heel, walked swiftly over to his vehicle, jumped in and drove off.

The next day, he parked in a different spot and went about his day. One call after the other came in for grass fires. The firefighters were run ragged. It was that time of the year when the thaw was over and the grass dried out from the deep winter frost and spring sunshine. The only way to beat it was with back fires and then that wasn't always successful. Unfortunately one barn was lost. Watson made a mental note to hold seminar on grass fires as soon as possible.

The chief made his way to his car; he was tired, and had more on his mind than a drip of oil. As he drove away, he noticed a sizeable spot of oil on the ground where he had been parked. Irate, he drove away hastily, directly toward the Oldsmobile dealership.

He entered the sales office and found the salesmen who had sold him the car.

"That bloody car is leaking oil!" he shouted, pointing out the window towards his car. His face was puffed red with anger.

"Can't be," said the salesman. "It's brand new."

"It has leaked oil from the first day I bought it! If you want to come back with me to the parking lot at the station, I'll show you the proof!"

"That won't be necessary. Just give it one more shot; see what happens tomorrow then call me. If need be, we'll replace it."

Two days later Garth pulled into the parking lot, parked his car and was walking toward the front door when he saw Chief Watson drive in. Was he seeing things? Did the chief have a different car? The new one he had last week was white, this one was black.

"Morning, Chief," he said smiling. "Nice car you have there."

"Yeah, the last one kept leaking oil so they exchanged it for me. This one better not do that or there'll be holy hell to pay."

Garth walked into the kitchen and took a place at the table where a gab session was in full force. Sean O'Sullivan was at the tail end of a joke and was laughing so hard he could hardly deliver the punch line. He got up and washed his cup, put it in the cupboard and then gazed out the window.

"There's a new black car in the parking lot. I wonder who owns that one."

"It belongs to the chief; the other one was leaking oil. Strange bit of business for a new car, I'd say," said Garth.

"Oh, so he had to exchange it. That would have been a hassle for him, wouldn't you say?" said O'Sullivan, his eyes twinkling.

He turned and left the room thinking that the time had come for him to stop squirting oil under the chief's car. Now that he had had his revenge, it was time to call it quits. It had gone a mite further than he'd intended. Besides, it was quite difficult putting the oil under such a big car, even with the long-spouted oil can.

Garth noticed Captain O'Sullivan was smiling when he left the room.

Cockroach!

***

He sat pensively on his bunk thinking about his job and his future. He'd been on the job nine months now, passed his probation period and had had time to consider whether he wanted to make it a career. There was no doubt in his mind that he would. He loved the thrill of knowing he was helping to save lives, and relished the camaraderie of his fellow workers, whose antics may have been foolish, yet when called upon to perform their duty, they took their work seriously.

He thought of the training session and his altercation with Hawks and although he did not regret landing the well-deserved punch, he wished he hadn't begun his career with extended probation. Garth thought about his very first call out to the river and how the arm came off the body. The men at the station had fun teasing him about that one. And he reflected on the first fire he attended, which was still fresh in his mind. It had been a Saturday night and thirty below zero. He had tucked an extra pair of mitts in an inside pocket and wore heavy socks. The horn had sounded for a three-alarm fire near the station at a building supply warehouse. He ran to the rig, donned boots and slicker, hooked the straps of his air supply on tightly and took out his mask.

When leaving the hall, he could immediately smell the rancid odour of smoke in the air; that always put the stamp of reality on his occupation as a firefighter. Garth put on his helmet, strapping it tightly under his chin as they raced down the highway.

Upon arriving at the scene he had donned his mask, turned on his air supply and went to the door of the building. A member of the pump crew handed him a nozzle and charged the line.

Garth opened the door and was met with what felt like a blast from a furnace, a burst of smoke and flames shooting in every direction. He opened the nozzle and sprayed in a circular motion, and had felt someone pushing him into the building from behind. It was a captain from another station, who was assisting him with the heavy hose. There was the colour of red everywhere. The water didn't make a squat of difference; it turned into hot steam before it hit the fire. The steam landed on his back and escaped beneath his slicker, scalding his neck and back, making it unbearable!

It took all Garth's effort to hang onto the nozzle and he couldn't back up, he was pinned in place by the captain behind him. His only hope was to keep spraying and try to control the flames, but he was terrified and felt as though he would be incinerated from the inferno.

Training had taught him never to let go of the nozzle, no matter what. The forward pressure released and Garth could feel the captain pulling the hose back. Finally, they exited the building and were met by the fresh, cool air.

Garth had gone over to the rig, exchanged his air bottle and sat down on a retaining wall to catch his breath. His neck was raw but he was prepared to soldier on. He had heard the deafening sound of paint cans exploding on the third floor and had wondered what else was in there.

"You two go around to the rear and relieve the crew in the stairwell on the second floor. Try to gain access to the second floor. Stay safe," said the captain.

They had climbed the rear stairway dragging the hose to the second floor and entered with a straight stream shooting. There were cans, cinders and sparks flying everywhere. What a rush! All the training in the world couldn't have prepared them for this excitement!

Soon, they were by accompanied by another group of firefighters, who made a sweep towards the front making attempts to keep the water high so as to flush everything out of the window. When the bells on their air supply had gone off, they were forced to retreat in order to get a new supply.

The attack had gone on for several hours before it was brought under control. At nightfall, each floor was patrolled with flashlights in order to extinguish any sparks or hot spots. Garth's clothing had been ringing wet, and now with the heat of fire dissipating, he had to jump up and down to keep warm in the frigid weather. Daylight brought relief, and they were allowed to return to the station. Unfortunately, however, Garth wasn't allowed to go home. He had to be admitted to the hospital for treatment of the burns on his neck and back.

As he sat on his bed, he recalled how his curiosity had been satisfied and now knew what being a firefighter was all about. Back then he'd wondered if he would get trapped in a confined space, have to search for victims and listen to cries for help from those he couldn't reach.

Garth remembered the first car accident that he had been called to; teenagers had been drag racing on 10th Avenue, and it had been reported they must have been drinking. One vehicle ran flush into a parked gravel truck at close to one hundred miles an hour. Their vehicle had been reduced to a mangled ball of metal buried beneath the truck and it took several hours to retrieve it. Amongst the carnage, the bodies were unrecognizable.

Garth had been unable to sleep that night. Images of the accident and the remains of body parts had been too much for him to bear. Finally, when daylight came, he hadn't slept a wink.

Now, Garth had no doubts about what the job entailed. He was no longer daunted and was ready and willing to face whatever new challenges would come his way.

CHAPTER

8

CHIEF WATSON SAT DRUMMING HIS FINGERS ON HIS desk. The time had come for him to select next year's calendar. He was proud of the funds raised from sporting events for the local burn unit at the hospital, but it was the firefighter calendar that brought in the most money and publicity.

He had enhanced the method of choosing just the right men and worked hard at making the event a celebration by concluding the final selection with a dinner and dance. Usually, there were about twenty-five men who had the courage to put their name forth, but the twelve that made the cut definitely walked with heads held a little higher.

Garth had first noticed the ad about the calendar posted on the bulletin board when he was checking the shift roster. He knew it would be the subject of discussion at the coffee table that morning.

Captain O'Sullivan was front and centre of the conversation. When asked if he would compete, he puffed up his chest and said, "But, of course, can't have these muscles hidden from the ladies forever. Just think of what they'd be missing." With that he flexed his right arm stretching the sleeve with his bicep.

"Their eyes won't get past that shiny dome of yours. Maybe you should get a wig," said Drew. The amateur photographer sat at the far end of the table. Laughter rippled around.

O'Sullivan had got past the teasing for his baldness, so he gave little credence to Drew's remark.

"Hey, Winters, are you going into the show?"

Garth smiled and looked around the table. They were all waiting pensively for his reply.

"Hell, I hadn't given it any thought," he replied, smiling and feigning a cough. In fact, he had been thinking it would be a hoot, and a chance to get the attention of the lady cop he had found attractive.

"You'll get a lot of lady admirers," said O'Sullivan. "Last year, when I was Mr. January, my phone rang off the hook."

"Bull," said Drew, not realizing one should never take on O'Sullivan without expecting some bruising.

"Looks like you're having a little problem today, Sonny boy. I'd hate like hell to see your skinny carcass on the calendar," retorted the captain. "Hell, they'd have to shut the fire station down."

Laughter erupted and continued for several minutes.

With a face ten shades of crimson, Drew got up, washed his cup and put it back in the cupboard. The captain had touched a sore spot. He'd been exercising on a regular basis to try and build up his physique, and was now so embarrassed by the captain's words. He had been forced to leave the room.

Garth watched Drew leave and thought, *No love lost between those two.*

*** *** ***

"I understand you're pretty handy with the camera," said Chief Watson, hoping his compliment would be effective.

Drew sat in front of his desk squirming. He'd wondered why the chief had summoned him and had thought the worst. Perhaps O'Sullivan had filed a complaint of insubordination against him. He was relieved to discover that had not been the case.

"Yes, I do quite a bit photography for family and friends, and for my own pleasure."

"I'm looking for a slide show for the upcoming calendar selection. Normally, we have the men model and they are selected by the applause, but this year I'm going to do things differently for a change. There are twenty-five men you'll have to photograph. Then we'll have a slide show at a dinner and dance evening with a selection made for each of the calendar months. They will be chosen by secret ballot. We always start with the month of January. That being the first page of the calendar, it's the one that holds the most prestige."

"When do you want these pictures taken?" asked Drew.

"Just do it at your convenience. However, try to have them done within the next couple of weeks and work it around their shifts. Here is a list of those competing. Oh, and another thing," said the chief with his eyebrows raised. "Would you be able to act as the master of ceremonies for the voting part of the evening?"

Drew could see that the chief was expecting him to decline. Having been a Toastmaster and an actor at a small local theatre, what had made him believe that Drew was an experienced public speaker? Those credentials were not necessary for a firefighter but were certainly coming in handy today.

"I'd be happy to do that," he replied while thinking, *there's more to me than a skinny body putting the wet stuff on the red stuff,* an expression used by firefighters meaning water on fire.

Watson handed the list to Drew and was smiling broadly when he said, "Thanks, man, this is much appreciated. Just let me know any costs that you have to incur. The department will reimburse you."

Drew took the list and stood up beaming. "You're welcome, Sir." The left the chief's office feeling proud that he had been selected for such an important task.

Back at his room he looked over the list. As expected O'Sullivan was at the top of the list and at the very bottom was Garth Winters, someone he greatly admired for a number of reasons. In particular, he respected the fact that he never boasted about anything, and when he spoke, it was always with logic. One thing Drew knew for sure was that the pompous O'Sullivan was going to be the last one he would schedule.

The next day it was Drew Anderson's day off. He had checked his camera equipment and it was in great shape, so he only needed to buy some film. As he backed his car out onto the street, he had to shield his eyes from the bright sun casting its rays between feathery clouds.

He felt exhilarated to be given such an important assignment. First, he would drop by the station to get a copy of last year's calendar to see how he could better it, along with the shift roster which contained the phone numbers of the twenty-five competitors. This was going to be so much fun and he was going to make it the best calendar ever. Thoughts were whirling around in his head faster than the wheels on a fire truck.

One by one he called the men in for a photo shoot. Some shots were posed by the fire truck, others holding the large hose with one leg up on a ladder. They were all in swim trunks with their flexed, muscular biceps, hairy chests and rippled thigh and abdominal muscles on full display. To give significance to these risqué photos, all wore a part of their fire-fighting gear and, of course, a proud leering-type grin.

As planned, O'Sullivan was the last man he called in and, as expected, he wouldn't cooperate. Getting him to pose a certain way was like pulling teeth from a snake. Finally, Drew put his camera down and shouted, "Listen here, daddy-o, this is my turf and if you won't follow my direction, you can miss being on the calendar altogether." That did the trick. O'Sullivan yielded to Drew's instruction and the shoot was quickly over.

But it wasn't over for Drew; he could still feel the sting from the coffee room remark. A plan began to formulate in his head and the more he thought about it, the more it became a reality. He was chuckling out loud in his car all the way back to his residence.

The shooting of the photos was the easy part. Compiling everything and planning the show proved more of a challenge. But Drew was on a mission. He spent considerable time finding perfect seasonal pictures to superimpose for each calendar month, and once the men were chosen, he would use these for the background. For entertainment value he decided to keep everything on a high note, interjecting humour at every possible turn. After all, wasn't a cheesecake picture of a firefighter the epitome of humour? And weren't the voyeuristic people attending the party expecting to be fully entertained?

He could hardly wait to be the emcee of the event.

The weather couldn't be more perfect for the event being held at the local arena. Like previous years, a sizable crowd was expected. But this year, ticket sales had broken all records.

Chief Watson was keeping a close eye on the numbers to keep within the city's fire regulations. Presently, the hall was at safe capacity.

A long white-skirted food table was erected down the centre of the dance floor, which was laden with food. It was a feast for the eyes and the big appetites in the room.

A band was set up on the stage with a banner spread that read: "The Country Boys". At the front of the stage on the floor was a large, white screen adjacent to a projector which sat on a small table.

Drew sat near the front wearing his best suit and best per-petual smile. He looked around the room at all the firefight-ers and his eyes came to rest on Garth Winters, who caught his glance and nodded.

Garth was strikingly handsome, wearing a black suit with blue shirt and tie. Seated with a couple of other loners, he glanced across the table at another firefighter, the only one who had a date seated beside him.

She was introduced as Kyla Jones from City Hall. Garth couldn't keep his eyes off her and therefore was no longer interested in the lady cop. The attraction to this brunette was immediate. She spoke softly and laughed spontaneously; something he appreciated in a woman. Her smile always reached her chocolate eyes first—eyes with a million lights in them and as clear as the prairie sky. They were eyes filled with so much promise! Her glossy, dark hair that hung to her shoulders contrasted beautifully with her peaches and cream complexion.

While Garth had always preferred blondes, tonight a brunette had changed his mind entirely. She was wearing a dark red dress with the front just low enough to see a hint of cleavage. He stole furtive glances there and he was aroused. It had been far too long since having the company of a woman. He wondered if she felt as good as she looked and he hoped to get a chance to dance with her. He looked at the firefighter who'd brought her and considered himself far better suited than that little rooster!

Garth looked at the screen in front of the stage and felt a little embarrassed at the thought that this attractive lady would see him in his swim trunks.

Why did I let them talk me into it?

The meal progressed along with idle talk at the table. Garth commented, "Isn't this roast beef great? And the gravy couldn't be better. It's almost as good as my mother's."

Kyla's date responded: "I'm going up for seconds."

The man stood up with plate in hand and strutted with a swagger like he was the cock on the walk toward the food table. No doubt he was feeling arrogant because he was with a beautiful woman. He hadn't asked her if *she* wanted more, though. Clearly the man had no manners. Garth wondered why she would accept a date with him.

"Have you been working at City Hall a long time, Kyla?" enquired Garth, admiring her brown eyes.

"That depends what you call long," she laughed. It was music to his ears. "I went there directly from business college. It will be five years in November."

"You must like it there or you wouldn't stay," said Garth, and as an after-thought added, "I bet City Hall likes you."

She felt the warmth of his words and didn't respond. Instead, she simply smiled, showing a stock of perfectly white teeth.

Damn it, she's pretty. Oh shit, here comes the rooster back to the table. His plate was piled high.

A whistle indicated someone was about to speak.

"Ladies and gentlemen, for those who don't know me, I am Chief Hadley, and I would like to welcome you once again to the Firefighters' Annual Calendar Ball. We are happy to see so many of you out this evening in support of this worthwhile cause. I understand we have a capacity crowd, and as you know all the proceeds from this evening go to the burn unit at the children's hospital. To date we have given over one-hundred thousand dollars to the hospital and will be adding more from this evening's event and from the sale of the calendars. I would like to ask District Chief Watson to stand and receive thanks for putting this evening together." Watson stood up smiling broadly and nodded to the applause.

"And let's put our hands together for the fine meal the caterers prepared for us.

"Last, but as they say 'not least', we have to thank the firefighters; the good sports that they are. Without them, we wouldn't be here tonight and wouldn't be able to give our help to the children's burn unit at the hospital."

When the applause was over, he continued: "I am happy also to call upon Drew Anderson, firefighter from Station No. 5. He will be acting as master of ceremonies and conducting the selection. Drew is also a photographer and has taken all the pictures, which will be presented to you via a slide show."

Drew, assisted by another firefighter, carried the large screen near the audience, closing the expanse of the dance floor. They spent a little time raising it high enough to give everyone good view.

Drew took the microphone from the chief and addressed the audience. "Thank you, Chief. I'm happy to have been given this interesting task. I've been a master of ceremonies for weddings, anniversaries and other social gatherings, but this . . . this is the first time I'll be conducting a . . . beauty pageant."

He threw back his head and laughed and was given a round of applause from the audience. The mood was set.

"Ladies and gentlemen, you have a big job ahead of you selecting the Calendar Boys. It will be conducted by secret ballot. You will see a ballot box on each table containing your ballots with the names of the competitors numbering one to twenty-five. However, we can select only twelve because I believe there's twelve months in a year, or so I'm told. You must not put more than twelve check marks on your ballot paper.

"Also, the second column on your ballot will be for the January Boy, and there you will put only one check mark in the column beside your overall favourite. Any questions?"

"Yes?" Drew pointed to a man in the middle of the hall who shouted, "What is so special about the January Boy?"

"January has always been the most prestigious as it will be the cover of the calendar. The public are enticed by the cover to buy it just to see what other beauties lie within."

The audience laughed and clapped.

"Alright, ladies and gentleman, let's get this show on the road."

Drew sat down at the table and began to operate the projector. The screen lit up and a most voluptuous blonde woman was projected on the screen. She was topless with only a couple of pasties over her nipples and a little fan over the apex of her thighs. She sprawled on a chaise lounge and her long golden tresses hung over, almost to the floor. There was a fat little cat sleeping on a lacy, pink pillow at her feet. She wore a Mona Lisa smile while one eye gave a flirtatious wink. She was definitely a rare and mischievous beauty.

Drew looked up and then jumped to his feet saying, "Oops, pardon me! Wrong slide!"

The audience thundered with laughter, wolf calls and whistles.

Drew flicked it off the screen and when the audience had spent its laughter, he continued with the firefighters. One by one they were displayed. Chief Watson was so impressed with the quality, he could hardly believe his eyes.

Garth sat at the table dreading his exposure on the screen when, almost at the end, there he was as big as life, all six feet of him standing in front of a pump in swim trunks with his legs casually crossed. All he wore of his bunker gear was his boots and hat. It was his smile that captivated everyone. He evoked a mix of seriousness of his career and sexual masculinity.

There was a gasp in the audience, and he hoped he had heard a hum of approval from Kyla. He stole a quick look at her and for a split second their eyes locked and something magic passed between them.

Finally, the twenty-fifth photo was displayed. It was O'Sullivan, who had been waiting all evening to see himself. Standing in front of a firefighter's ladder, he had one leg up on a garbage can and his arms were stretched out in a muscular pose. His face had been superimposed and every rib was showing above a caved-in stomach. His knees were knobby and bigger in circumference than his legs which were as thin as an ostrich's. The audience was laughing uproariously for what seemed like an eternity. Drew was laughing the hardest and thinking: *I've shown you what skinny is, you smart ass! Oh, sweet revenge!*

Aghast, O'Sullivan exclaimed, "What the fu—" He caught himself from completing the expletive just in time; there were ladies at the table.

It didn't take him long before he was on his feet and marching up to the front peeling off his shirt. When at the front by the screen he displayed his hairy chest and began flexing his muscles posing in different positions. He was blessed with broad shoulders and large biceps, his tattoos of the insignia at this moment added to his demeanour. The ladies in the room were screaming with delight, "Take it off, take it off, take it all off!"

He whipped off his belt, sucked in his abs making his waistband stand free. Then he hooked his thumbs in the belt loops and began sliding his trousers down when Chief Watson stepped in and put a stop to it, or one only knows how far he would have gone.

O'Sullivan put his shirt back on and when passing Drew gave him his best sneer, and a back-handed finger. He paused and with a toothy grin took a bow to the audience before heading back to his table while the applause continued.

Wearing a smile of satisfaction, Drew took the microphone, hushed the audience and requested everyone mark their ballots. While he was disgusted with O'Sullivan, he shrugged and said to himself, "Par for the course." He also realized the audience had never been so completely entertained by any previous Calendar Ball. It was a huge success.

"After your ballots are marked, they will be picked up and counted. Please enjoy the dance. You will be given the results of the vote at intermission."

Now, with the screen and projector put away, the band struck up its first waltz.

The melodious voice of the lead singer rang through the dance hall. The soft melody was in sharp contrast to the raucous past half-hour and its soothing effect on the audience brought them to the dance floor.

The words, which were so ironic, fell on Garth's ears in disbelief. He couldn't bring himself to look at Kyla but when he finally did, she was out on the dance floor with the rooster. This gave him a chance to advance his impressions, watch her dance, and check out her curvaceous figure. She definitely had rhythm and it was obvious her date did not. He stumbled along. Garth felt like tapping him on his shoulder and cutting in to put him out of his obvious misery. However, they managed to get through the dance, and when they returned to the table, he left her alone while he made his way to the bar. A snappy two-step replaced the waltz and she looked across at Garth. He was smiling and tapping his fingers on the table to the beat.

"Are you a dancing man?" she asked demurely while appraising his dark curly hair and astonishing blue eyes.

Garth nodded and was on his feet in an instant. He came around the table and pulled her chair. They walked out to the dance floor and he folded her into his arms. Remarkably they fell immediately in step.

He manoeuvred her around the dance floor feeling her softness and smelling her fragrance. They didn't speak; instead, they just danced in unison to the music. Every once in a while she would glance up and smile into his eyes, which made his heart beat faster. When the dance was over, he released her and took her back to the table, feeling bereft without her.

How can this be happening to me? I just met the lady.

Much to Garth's disappointment, her date danced with her the rest of the evening. Garth didn't have the opportunity to dance with her again, so he circulated around the tables to visit others he knew. He spotted Hawks at a nearby table.

Don't tell me he's here!

Seeing him aroused the memory of how his air was disconnected in the smoke house during training. That was nine months ago, yet the sight of him still had the power to bite into his gut.

Does his jaw look little out of balance, or is it is it my imagination?

The music had stopped and everyone returned to their tables, anxious to hear results. It was time for an intermission and Drew was quickly up onto the stage with microphone in hand.

"Ladies and gentlemen, can I have your attention please. We now have the results of the competition that you've all been waiting for. As I call out the twelve successful candidates, I want the candidates to come up to the stage for a group photo. So, please hold your applause until all the successful candidates are on the stage. Those who haven't made the cut can go home and cry in their beer. Just kidding; you're all winners today."

As the names were called, twelve men lined up on the stage. Garth and O'Sullivan were amongst them.

"Ladies and gentlemen," Drew announced, "here are your Calendar Men!"

The audience thunderously clapped their approval then Drew positioned them in two rows of six and snapped their picture. Then, he announced it was time to reveal the January Boy.

"It is a unanimous decision. The man receiving the land-slide vote is . . . Sean O'Sullivan."

The audience were on their feet clapping.

All Drew could say was, "Oh Well!" Although he had hoped for Garth to win, he didn't care one iota that O'Sullivan had taken it. He had something much greater of which to be proud. Didn't Chief Watson shake his hand and say? "Well done, Drew!" So, why should he care if the pompous jackass O'Sullivan won January? He shouldn't care a whit. After all, he'd made his mark and was a happy man when he gathered up his equipment to head off home.

Garth was disappointed that the evening had finally come to an end. Saying goodbye to Kyla was difficult. However, with discretion, she handed him her social card, which he slipped into his breast pocket and gave it a light pat to show his approval.

CHAPTER

9

GARTH WAS HAPPY TO HAVE FOUR DAYS OFF AND TIME to go riding on Nellie, his old horse. He galloped around his acreage dreaming of where he'd one day build his home. He hoped it would be soon. Living in the small apartment he now occupied tested his patience more than once. His only consolation being that he knew it was temporary.

He gazed across the land imagining a rancher-type home painted white with a red, tiled roof. He also imagined lovely green shrubbery and a garden patch with rows so even people visiting would comment and he'd reply, "Just two sticks and a string."

He kept Kyla's card in his wallet, checking frequently to make sure it was still there. He would think of her often, yet he didn't want to call her too soon; the three-day wait, seemed in his opinion, most prudent. They had met on Saturday, and now that it was Wednesday, so the three days were up. The time had come to work up the courage to call her for a date. But, what if she said no?

She wouldn't have given me her card if she wasn't interested, he thought.

Pacified by this thought, he decided he'd call her as soon as he got back to his apartment.

Her voice was sweet and perky over the telephone and his deep and hesitant.

"Hey, Kyla, it's me."

"And I should know who me is?" she queried, giving out a little giggle.

"I can hope," he replied.

"And I can hope it might be Garth."

"Bingo!"

She laughed again melodiously. "How are you, Garth? I'm so happy you're calling."

Damn it, she sounds so nice! "When can we get together, Kyla? I was wondering about your date at the dance, if he'd mind."

"Oh, him. He's just a co-worker. I'm free on Saturday. We can go to a dance if you'd like. There's one on at the Old Stone Inn."

"You have my vote. And where might I find you?"

It took Kyla a few seconds to realize he was unconventionally asking for her address: "Oh, I live at 76 Morley Street, apartment nine."

"Great," he said. "I'll pick you up at 7:30. See you then."

When Garth hung up the phone, he was elated. It had been a long time since he had dated a woman. He had been so busy trying to establish a career that he just didn't have a time to think about it. But since meeting Kyla, the strong attraction that captivated his thoughts and aroused his feelings so completely forced him to think of little else. How long would it take to get to know her—really know her? Wednesday to Saturday was going to take an eternity.

When Kyla hung up the phone, she closed her eyes and placed her hand on her chest. She could see his dark curly hair and steely blue eyes and her heart quickened like it had done so at the calendar party on Saturday. When their eyes met at the table they had then danced without the need for any conversation.

Oh, what'll I wear? How should I fix my hair? Oh! Oh! she wondered.

***

When Garth approached Morley Street, everything looked beautiful. Early evening sunrays gilded chimney corners and, as they slanted down between the tall cedars, gave birth to long shadows on the sidewalk. He drove around the block twice looking for the address; the numbers were partly concealed with ivy.

If there should be a fire, we would be hard pressed to find it quickly. I must discuss this with Chief Watson.

The lobby of the apartment building, though fairly old, was nicely maintained. A stuffed floral sofa placed beneath the lace-covered window invited one to sit and perhaps read a while from the many books on display in the adjacent bookcase.

Garth rang the bell to apartment nine and waited patiently. When she opened the door he smiled, enamoured by her beauty. "Looks like I have the right apartment," he said, still smiling as he admired her off-the-shoulder red dress.

She laughed. "What was your first clue?" Not waiting for his answer she said, "Come in and make yourself at home. I'll only be a minute."

As she turned and walked down the hall, he noticed her slim figure, shapely legs and the gentle curve of her hips. He moved across the simply furnished room to look at the photographs displayed on the fireplace. Pictures of older people he reckoned were relatives, and one that he was sure must have been her graduation picture. The one on the far corner of the mantle held his attention. It was a man sat on what looked like an Allis Chalmers tractor, holding a little, dark-haired girl on his lap. He wondered if it was Kyla.

"That's my father," she said from behind him. "I was three years old when that picture was taken. I loved riding with him on old Sadie. That's what he called the tractor."

"Did you grow up living on a farm?" he asked.

"Yep, and loved it. But now I'm a city gal. I like it here too, but someday I'll probably go back to the farm where nature dictates, not alarm clocks, city buses, sirens and such like. Give me the crowing of rooster, chirping of the birds and a meal made fresh from the garden and I will be happy."

She beamed him a smile which made his heart quicken. Her voice was like music to his ears.

"I feel the same way, Kyla, but life can be hard on the farm. Only folks that take things in their stride, and learn to live off the land, eventually succeed."

"You sound like a farmer, Garth, not a firefighter."

"Actually I'm both. I do have some land in the country, which I hope to develop some day."

"Good for you, Garth. I guess we should head off to the dance."

She took her coat from the closet; he helped her put it on and they headed out the door. Everything seemed so natural and right.

The Old Stone Inn was several blocks away. As its name suggested, the building was old and the front of the inn was faced with cut stones of different sizes and colours. A mosaic held together with plaster. The front double-doors were oval-shaped and had levers instead of door knobs . . . the finishing touch to the building's outdated appearance.

When they stepped inside, they were greeted by the sound of lively music. Garth could see that the inside of the building was more modern than its exterior in every respect. Kyla tapped her feet to the beat of the music as Garth paid their entrance fee. On the stage was a combo of three musicians; one on drums, another on bass, and the third strumming his guitar and rhythmically slapping the strings between notes. The sound was upbeat, lending itself to Garth's favourite, a two-step.

They found a table and sat down. Across the room were other couples sat at tables. By the bar stood three young men ogling the single women at every opportunity. Garth wondered if Kyla knew them.

"Would you like something to drink?" he asked.

"Water with a twist of lemon would be great."

He walked over to the bar and while waiting for their drinks, turned and looked across the room at her sitting alone at the table. He knew if he wasn't with her those young bucks at the bar would be pouncing on her like stallions after a mare. With that thought in mind, he hurried back to the table and put her drink before her and extended his hand, "Shall we?"

The man on the guitar had begun singing 'The Tennessee Waltz' in a relaxed, baritone voice. They glided around the dance floor like they had been dancing together all their lives. She felt so good in his arms; everything about her felt good. She danced well and the perfume from her hair was intoxicating. She was just the right height. He could look over her head and when she looked up at him with her big brown eyes, he almost lost his step.

This must be what love feels like. I hope this bubble doesn't burst. Should I tell her how I feel? No, it might scare her away. I must make another date with her right away. I wonder if she likes to ride. I could show her my land. I have to get to know her, really know her.

When they returned to their table he asked: "Do you like to ride?"

"I presume you mean horses," she laughed. "And not the merry-go-round. Yes, I love riding. I used to have my very own horse. Actually, I still have it but it's at my parents' house on the farm; getting kind of old now."

"Would you like to go riding tomorrow?" he asked.

"I'd love to." Her eyes brightened with excitement.

"I have a nice little mare that needs some exercise," said Garth.

"What will you ride?"

"A gelding called Jake. He's sixteen hands and goes like a hot damn."

"Does that mean you'll canter while I gallop?"

He threw back his head and laughed. "Heck no, that little mare can keep up to Jake, I'm sure."

"What's her name?"

"She doesn't have one. Perhaps you can name her for me."

"OK, I'll do that tomorrow after I ride her. This is going to be fun. I've never had a chance to name someone else's horse."

They danced for the remainder of the evening, enjoying each other's company, and in the knowledge that they would ride together the following day. Kyla was equally impressed with Garth. He made her feel wonderful. She couldn't help but notice how nicely groomed he was, how clean he smelled and how his eyes shone when he looked at her. Yes, he made her feel wonderful.

Could this be love? she wondered. *Much too soon, much too soon to know.*

Back at her apartment door, he smiled but made no attempt to kiss her. She wondered if he would. He wanted to. He wanted to gather her in his arms and feel her lips on his. It was a painful restraint on his part. But he didn't want to be too quick with things, as he wanted to give her the respect she deserved, and he wanted her to know that. Yet, he wasn't going to wait forever. Tomorrow they would be together again. Maybe he'd kiss her then; maybe tomorrow he would fulfil his longing.

"Thanks for a wonderful time," she said standing in the doorway.

"Thank *you*," he replied. "It was most enjoyable. See you tomorrow." He gave her a little salute which she found so appealing.

That night, Kyla tossed and turned in bed for a short time before finally drifting off to sleep.

When morning came, she woke up in a state of bliss, excited for the day ahead. She was going riding with Garth.

When Kyla took the reins, stepped in the stirrups and swung up into the saddle, the little mare was gentle and receptive to its new rider. She was pleased and Garth thought she looked at home astride the mare. He found her desirable in tight-fitting blue jeans and matching jacket. Her dark hair was gathered back with a red polka-dot bandana holding it in place.

Kyla thought Garth looked so handsome as he sat on his horse. She rode alongside him and then they walked their horses amongst the tall cedars down the lane. The earthy smell of the forest was intoxicating.

"Whoa," said Garth drawing on the reins. Kyla followed suit. "Once we get through these woods there is a nice open trail where we can trot and gallop the horses. What is your preference?"

"I'll trot her for a while then I'd love to gallop at full speed if you think that's OK."

"Perhaps you should hold her back a bit for safety sake; this is the first time you're riding her and I wouldn't want anything to happen to you. She's from racing stock and will go like a bullet." After all, he had not seen her ride and didn't know her capabilities.

Kyla laughed. "Thanks for your concern, Garth. I won't give her full rein."

They came to a large, open field yellowed with canola. An inviting path cut across it as far as the eye could see. They clucked, "Giddy up" and the horses were off; trotting at first then breaking into a loping gallop. Both were exhilarated as the fall air flowed against their faces. He could hear her laughter as the pace picked up, and he could see how natural she was on the horse; she was without doubt an accomplished rider. She was a picture beauty and excitement. Riding was a respite from all that transpired at the fire station, and riding now with Kyla, made him feel the utmost contentment.

But what will happen next? That thought occupied his mind. He saw a small grove of trees up ahead and brought his horse to a halt. Kyla did likewise and laughed, "Are you all worn out, Mr. Winters?"

He enjoyed her joyful and teasing nature. He alighted from his horse and went over to her and offered to help her down. She accepted and once free of the stirrups, slid slowly down the front of him. Automatically, his arms were around her, holding her against him. He could feel her warm breath on his neck. His lips pressed against the top of her head, then her forehead, then he explored her face with feathery kisses before coming to a crushing rest upon her lips. To his joy she had melted in his arms with a response that matched his ardour. They believed that their first kiss had ended too soon. Kyla opened her eyes and looked into his.

"What am I going to do about you, Mr. Winters?"

"Can I take you to dinner tonight?"

"Yes," she whispered breathlessly.

CHAPTER

10

GARTH WINTERS WAS IN LOVE. NO DOUBT ABOUT IT.
There was a brand new joy in his life by the name of Kyla. He
awoke each morning with a good feeling and went to bed
with equal excitement. The world around him now took on
a new glow—everything seemed much rosier. He thought
of Kyla every waking minute of the day and dreamt about
her all night long. He found himself reliving every little frag-
ment of conversation they had shared.

She was everything and more of what he wanted in a
woman: solid character, happy personality, pretty face, nice
figure, loved country living, and was a great rider too. Not
that riding was all important but it was a bonus, something
they could share. He loved the way she tilted her head giving
him a long side glance when in doubt of what he was saying.

He loved her mannerisms, the way she used her hands
to punctuate her sentences. But most of all he valued how

loving she was toward him, making him feel like the most important person on Earth. Yes, he was in love and more grateful than ever to have a steady job and land upon which he could build a home.

The only missing spoke in his wheel of contentment was a question that kept nagging him: *Did she feel the same way?* It was much too soon to broach the subject with her; he didn't want to scare her away. He just had to be patient and bide his time and stay close in case someone else came along and scooped her away. They had another date that evening to see a movie.

Because she was constantly in his thoughts, he had to force himself to keep his mind on his job. Now, as he sat with the guys at the infamous table, hub of the station, it was almost incongruous that he should be there. He felt out of place, as no one else was in the state of euphoria as he. They were, however, all dedicated firefighters, who were faithfully serving their community. After one year on the job, Garth learned how dedicated they all were, and as the days passed, his admiration for his fellow firefighters only grew.

He also learned that as the city of Papillon expanded, new fire stations were required to service the new districts and to relieve the burden on ones already established. This brought a number of rookie firefighters to the scene who were in need of training. They gained experience by being partnered with seasoned firefighters when a call came in. Some would come without the bravery needed to enter a burning building; they would just stand back and hold the door open for someone else to enter first. The crew called them the Door Men. They never lasted long.

Others arrived on the job thinking they could do everything. But, if they could not handle the cutting torch for extrication or operate other lifesaving equipment, they soon found themselves delegated to driving the rigs. They learned, when driving, accidents and near accidents could easily happen. Surprisingly the occurrence of such accidents was few.

Garth soon learned how important it was to keep harmony among the men who were working in close proximity during the long shifts. Being angry with one another over some silly dispute at the coffee table was not conducive to success on the job. They all knew this; and while things could often become intense between them, they were quick to put aside their differences.

Garth sat at the coffee table amused as he listened to the men unravel their stories like yarn from a ball of wool. They were chatting about their escapades and, whether they happened to be true of not, they would laugh out loud as they told their tale. This was their way of dealing with the challenges of the job.

Holding a cup of coffee, Charlie Morgan began to recount what had happened to him and Johnny Baxter the previous week: "We were down in the south end after a call. It was ten o'clock in the evening. We were heading back to the station when we passed a gay bar.

"'Let's go in.' I said.

"Johnny said, 'Are you kidding? We can't do that. We're in uniform and you know the rules.'

"'Oh come on,' I said. 'I'd love to be able to tell my wife when I get home, she'll never believe me. Let's go in and do a quick dance across the floor, just for fun.'

At this point he looked over at a smiling Johnny who was enjoying the rendition of their caper.

Charlie continued: "Johnny could finally see the humour and fun in it and agreed. We parked the fire engine by the front door and went inside. When we walked in, I'm sure the gay crowd inside thought there must have been an alarm. Why else would two uniformed firefighters come in? The band had just struck up a two-step so Johnny and I danced a fast side-step across the floor. This infuriated the manager, he charged after us shouting, 'Get, get out or I'll call the police.'

"We took a quick bow and ran out to the truck with several chasing after us."

Upon hearing this story, the men around the table were in stitches. Garth chuckled as he conjured up the mental image of two brawny firefighters in full uniform galloping in their rubber boots across the floor of a gay bar. The silly asses.

"I have to tell you what happened to me yesterday," said one of the older guys. "You're damn lucky to see me here today. I was called out to a car on fire at the north end of town. It was totally engulfed in flames. Let me tell you something: don't ever try to put cold water on hot head-lights. They both exploded—KABOOM—one after the other right in front of me. If I'd have been one foot closer, shit, I could've been killed. I've never seen anything like it. My ears are still ringing."

"Just common sense," said another, "but one just wouldn't think of it when putting a car fire out."

Garth was still chuckling over the gay bar story when a call came in loud and clear.

"Station 5 and 6, call to an apartment fire at 2045 Argyle Street!"

Garth's heart quickened.

"That would be me," he said rising quickly.

"Me too," said Charlie following suit.

Within one minute, both were speeding down the road towards Argyle Street with sirens wailing and the air horn ordering vehicles out of the way.

As their destination drew nearer, they could see the north sky had turned orange and there was billowing dark smoke beneath it. When they arrived at the site, they saw the fourth floor was almost engulfed with flames and several firefighters were already spraying the building.

A large crowd had gathered at the scene. However, a policeman was trying to console and hold back a woman who was crying hysterically and screaming, "My son's in there, my son's in there."

Garth quickly discovered the woman's four-year-old son was on the top floor. He'd locked himself in the bathroom when the fire alarm went off. She had run to the elevator but it was inoperable, so she scampered down four flights of stairs to the manager's office on the first floor for help, but he didn't answer the door and she couldn't get back up the stairs due to the heavy smoke.

Garth and Charlie hastily made their way up the ladder, which had been raised to the window of the woman's apartment. The heat was intense and the smoke heavy as they entered through the window. Groping their way around the wet apartment, amidst the stench and din, they were barely able to detect a door as they performed a systematic search. Garth found the locked bathroom door and with brute force kicked it in. There was no sign of the young boy anywhere. On a hunch, he pulled back the shower curtain and there lying face down was the body of a small boy. He turned him over and rushed to the window to give him oxygen. Almost immediately, Garth felt a hint of movement in the little body so he knew he was alive.

The smoke was intensifying so he hollered to Charlie, "Over here, over here!" Charlie hurried over to Garth. Flames began to lick up behind them, and with little visibility available to them, they eventually made their way to the window. Garth held the child firmly as the men began their descent. They removed their oxygen masks and the fresh air greeted him like a breeze across the meadow. It was a long way down to the bottom and hastily manoeuvring the wet rungs one after the other was an arduous effort. Garth spoke calmly to the child: "You're safe, buddy, you're safe."

Once on the ground, the boy's mother came rushing forward crying out, "Thank you, thank you, oh please God, let him live." Four ambulance attendants were right on her heels with a gurney. They quickly gathered the limp body from Garth and began performing CPR all the way to the waiting ambulance, which then sped off to the hospital. The wail of its siren could be heard for blocks around. Garth thought he'd heard a small voice calling out "Mama, Mama" but he couldn't be sure. Perhaps it was wishful thinking and his mind was playing tricks on him.

He sighed and smiled at the clapping crowd then headed back to the rig thinking: *This is the firefighter's reward.* On the way he passed a captain from another station who slapped him on the back saying, "Well done, man!"

As Garth was driving back to the station, he felt drained and found it hard to push the image of the fire out of his mind. He could still feel the little body in his arms and wondered if he had lived, and the sight of the wild-eyed, displaced tenants, some crying and holding what little memorabilia they had managed to save that day, hung in his mind.

After returning the apparatus to the station, and with his shift over, he headed home and decided he would rest a while before going to the show with Kyla.

As he unlocked the door of his apartment, he could hear his phone ringing. It was Kyla telling him what was playing at the Odeon; it was a movie they both wanted to see.

There was certain restlessness to her tone. He could tell she was struggling to tell him something else. He waited. A few seconds passed before she spoke again: "Oh, Garth, thank God for firefighters. I've just got off the phone with my cousin. Her little boy, Johnny was saved today in a fire on Argyle Street . . . saved just in the nick of time."

CHAPTER

11

THE FALL SEASON IN THE CANADIAN PRAIRIES COMES with a blaze of colour. Soft yellow and shades of orange and red can be seen in the few little groves that edge the flat lands. Flanked by a cerulean sky, this panorama of colour is contrasted sporadically by dark-green, coniferous trees. They stand tall like the guards of nature as though protecting the vista. But such wondrous sights have to be appreciated quickly, for all too soon the snow blows in, engulfing everything like a giant, white blanket; sometimes not giving the leaves on the little groves a chance to fully descend. Always there is the odd leaf fluttering against a stark branch.

Winter arrived earlier than normal for the time of the year, and Garth was knee deep in snow when he went out to his car. He ran the engine for a few moments making it easier to scrape the frost and snow off the windows.

It was Saturday afternoon and his day off. He was heading over to Kyla's. She had invited him to dinner. He had been thinking of nothing else but Kyla over the past few days.

He stopped off at the florist and bought a dozen red roses just to give her a hint of how much he cared, and if his courage didn't fail him, perhaps he would tell her tonight how he felt about her.

When she opened the door, he caught his breath. She was wearing a simple maroon dress—a colour that showed off her lovely complexion. She wore no jewellery except for little diamond drops at her ears.

A delicious smell was coming from the kitchen, making him realize how hungry he was. She smiled at him and he whispered, "Come here, you little darling." Garth held her in his arms and kissed her passionately before reaching for the roses that he had placed on a credenza near the door.

"My favourite," she said excitedly. "Thank you, Garth." She sniffed them and smiled, and then hurried into the kitchen to put them into a vase. He followed her and could see she had set a small table for dinner.

"Something smells good," he said, noticing the pots on the stove.

"Just stew and mashed potatoes, my good old standby. My mother always said, 'Can't go wrong with meat and

taters.' You strike me as a meat and potato type of guy."
She laughed.

"You got that right, Kyla, having lived most of my
life on the prairies, I've not had that much experience
with seafood."

"Well, now, I'm just going to have to change that and
make my infamous seafood Creole for you."

"You got my vote," he replied, grabbing her hand and
giving it a squeeze.

He used that phrase often to tell her he agreed and she
was always amused.

They sat down to a delicious meal. Garth couldn't
remember when he had ever enjoyed food as much. Her
cooking ability pleased him immensely and was added to
the long list of all the things he loved about her.

After the meal was over, Kyla quickly put the dishes in the
dishwasher then poured them each another glass of wine.

"Let's go into the living room and enjoy our wine,"
she said.

They walked out to the living room and Kyla placed
her wine on the coffee table and walked over to look out
the window.

"Come and see the Christmas lights on City Hall. We can see them from here. I love this time of year," she said.

Garth stood close behind her. She could feel his breath on the back of her neck, and then felt his hands slide under her arms and dangerously close to her breasts. "I love you, Kyla Jones," he said in a husky voice. After a dramatic pause, he whispered in her ear, "I want to make love to you."

He could feel her catch her breath. She turned around and her arms were instantly around his neck.

"But, Garth, we only just met three months ago. Only three months ago, darling."

He kissed her forehead gently: "It doesn't change how I feel. But I know you're right, sweet girl, you're right."

Be patient, be patient, Garth Winters!

Breaking the intensity of the moment, she asked, "Did you know the firefighter who saved Johnny?"

"Well, now," he replied. "Er, hum," he was searching for words, trying to say something without giving himself away.

Kyla was quick to recognize his awkwardness, his reticence. Her eyes grew large.

"Was it you? It *was* you! You're the one who saved my little cousin from that horrible fire? Our family is ever so grateful! Why didn't you tell me it was you, Garth Winters?"

"There was nothing to tell. I was just doing my job, Kyla, just doing my job."

She looked at him in wonder with grateful eyes and shook her head. The couple sat down on the sofa and Kyla nestled snugly into his arms while they watched a movie on the television. They laughed and shared the plot of the story, while both feeling comfortable in each other's presence.

The next day Garth walked into the coffee room to noisy chatter about the upcoming curling bonspiel, and where would one go to get a good Christmas tree.

"I know where we can go," said Charlie. "There's a guy I know, Jerry Smith, who lives out in the country. He was a firefighter for a while but left to take care of his ageing parents. He has great trees in the forest on his quarter section about fifteen miles from his house. I got mine there last year. I know we can cut down any tree we choose."

"That sounds great. Why don't we get a group of us together and head out there tomorrow," said Stanley.

"He loves his rum, so why don't we pick up some and make a party of it," replied Charlie.

"I wouldn't mind going. I could use a couple of trees," said Garth. He was thinking of giving one to Kyla and how much he'd enjoy a trip out to the countryside.

"My crew cab holds four so I can take one more," stated Charlie.

"I'm in," came from the far end of the table.

"Great," said Charlie. "We can all meet here tomorrow about noon. I'll give Jerry a call and if there are any changes I'll let you know."

"I'll pick up the rum," said Garth.

The next day was perfect for a trip out in the country. The sun was blazing off two solid feet of snow and the air was crisp—mighty crisp. All the men were dressed for the elements. Snow boots, scarves, toques, heavy winter coats and warm winter gloves.

Charlie was waiting with the motor on the crew cab running. The men climbed in and headed north down the snow-covered highway towards the Smiths' farm.

When they arrived at the farm they were greeted by Jerry, who came over to the cab window. "Just follow me," he said. "It might be a bit slow going, but shouldn't be too bad. I think they've cleared the roads since the last snowfall."

They followed Jerry passed several farms, when finally Jerry came to a stop at the end of a field where there was a large forested area. He got out of his truck and motioned to the men to follow him.

Leaving their vehicle in the clearing, Charlie made quick introductions, and then they trudged through the deep snow to the timbered area. Equipped with axes and small chainsaws they viewed the coniferous trees before them: white and black spruce, jack pine, balsam fir and tamarack larch. Soon they had sawed down their choices. They dragged them back and piled them in the back of the truck. Garth chose two six-foot jack pines with branches so dense, there wasn't even a hint of space between them.

Kyla will love one of these! he thought.

"Hey, guys, when we get back to the house, I'd like you all to come in for a cup of coffee," said Jerry.

"I can make that coffee, 'coffee-coffee'" said Garth. "I've brought some rum."

"All the better, that'll take the chill out of our bones."

When they walked through the door of Jerry's home, they were greeted by the strong smell of stale coffee and mustiness.

Garth was astounded. For him, the place held a touch of nostalgia; much of the furnishing was like that of his pioneering grandparents. The men were invited to sit at a wooden table in the centre of the room. The rosy-cheeked tree-cutters welcomed the steaming mugs of muddy coffee placed before them.

By the looks of it, it must have been sitting on the stove since early morning, thought Garth.

He was thankful for the rum to smooth it out and passed the flask around at the table.

An elderly gentleman came down the small staircase and joined them at the table. He was introduced by Jerry as his father. The six men sat around the table drinking their coffee and chatting about farming.

"Have you got much land here, Jerry?"

"Where you cut your trees is a quarter section, and here there's a full section."

"What do you sow?"

"Alfalfa, barley and canola. But mostly canola; had a good crop this year. Made up for last year, which was the pits. Got hailed out."

"I guess there's nothing much you can do with that quarter section as it stands now."

"That's true, it has to be cleared but I've been considering raising elk. I hear there's quite the market out there. They like woodland. It's much like their natural habitat."

"Elk, did you say? I would think cattle would be better."

"Did you know one cow takes five times more feed than one elk?"

"And something else," said Jerry, "there's a huge market in Japan for the velvet horns of elk. They use it as an aphrodisiac."

That little piece of information drew chuckles around the table.

"I've eaten elk and it was very tasty," said Garth.

"Did you eat meat or horns?"

Further laughter erupted around the table.

Garth smiled at him coyly and shelved his retort while thinking, Smartass!

"By the way," asked Charlie. "How's your mother doing, Jerry? She was under the weather last year when I visited."

"Oh, she's in the pump house. Do you want to see her?"

"Yes," he replied remembering how friendly she had been when he last visited. "And then we have to head back."

After donning their coats and boots, the men followed him across the yard in the deep snow to the pump house. Jerry unlocked the door with a skeleton key, which Garth considered unusual that the door should be locked if his mother was inside. They entered the small room and were met by a sweet odour mixed with the smell of straw. The men looked at one another apprehensively. They all had a creepy feeling.

Against one wall were several blocks of ice packed into a mound of straw and on top lay a wooden box with hinges made of leather. Jerry lifted the lid, and inside the box lay an elderly woman, obviously deceased. The men gasped.

Garth stood back. The last thing he wanted to see was someone's dead mother lying in a box on top of ice. But then he felt it might be offensive if he didn't step forward and take a look, so he did. She was laid out in a black dress with a white lace collar centred by a cameo. Her features were delicate, almost angelic and her hands clutched a small white bible. It was something one would expect to see in the movies. Ironically, her appearance was in keeping with the antiquity of the home.

Garth looked around the room at the disbelief on the guys' faces.

"She wanted to be buried on the farm next to her mother and dad. But the ground is frozen, so it will have to wait until spring," said Jerry.

"Isn't it against the law?" questioned Garth.

"Nope," said Jerry. "I checked it out. There's an old statute still on the books since 1928 that allows homesteaders to bury their family on their farms."

"Really, I didn't know that."

As they left the pump house the men thanked Jerry for his hospitality and for the trees, then headed for the truck. The men remained speechless for some time, when finally Charlie broke the silence: "I don't blame the guy. Doing it his way is a hell of a lot cheaper than dealing with a funeral home. I just hope that the pump house doesn't thaw out too much before the ground does." He smiled for being so witty.

The others offered their comments:

"Just imagine, living all winter knowing your mother lies dead in the pump house. I don't think I could do it."

"I think I'd have nightmares. God, that's the spookiest damn thing I've ever heard of!"

Garth shifted in his seat trying to make sense of it all while endeavouring to shake the image of the corpse from his mind's eye.

Kyla is going to be so shocked when I tell her about this. Maybe I won't. It might make her feel a little queasy about the tree. I'll tell her after Christmas.

CHAPTER

12

DISTRICT CHIEF WATSON SAT DEEP IN THOUGHT AT his desk, staring at the amber residue in the bottom of his coffee cup. He shifted his glance over to the big stack of calendars on his desk and then to the many boxes of them on the floor. Having ordered so many of them, he remained confident that after finding new market sources, he would sell every last one of them. He hoped to break all records and give the burn unit of the local hospital a bundle.

He took one from the top of the stack for perusal. There on the front stood the Alpha male, O'Sullivan, proudly standing in his swim trunks with his furry chest and one muscular leg cocked up on a fire hydrant. He had his right thumb hooked into his trunks while the other hand held the end of a fire hose supported by an arm of bulging muscles. A grin was pasted on his face like he was the epitome of every woman's dream, while a firefighter's hat sat a bit askew on his head.

The arrogant son of a bitch. If this doesn't sell calendars, nothing will. Yup, I'm going to break all records!

He thought about the trouble he'd had with O'Sullivan's tanning on the deck, and going to extreme by getting the insignia tattooed on both arms.

He's going to be surprised when I give him his orders to transfer to Station 3 today. I've had him now for two years. Time to pass him onto another district chief. Let someone else deal with the critter.

Watson also thought about what made a man join the fire department. He could never quite figure that out. He surmised some joined because the pay was good and for job security; others, because the shift-work with the many days off allowed them to have a second job. But in the end, he knew it was their dedication to their community and the strong desire to help others, which motivated them most. Wasn't that why *he* joined?

He continued to flip through the calendar, and stopped at the picture of Garth Winters.

Now there's a gentleman if ever there was one. I can see him going places within the department someday. He's definitely a cut above; a man to be trusted.

He'd heard the story about how Winters had stood up to Hawks when he had joined the service, and while it now seemed a mite out of character, he knew Winters was no pushover. He was a man with guts and just the type that was needed to lead the men.

Hmm, a man just like me; even if I do say so myself. He smiled at the absolute accuracy of his own self-analysis.

Meanwhile, down in the coffee room, word had already circulated regarding the possibility of a new captain. They all wondered who they'd get. The possibility of change brought the topic of officers to the table, especially when there were none present to hear their gossip. Today they were anxious to relate a funny incident with a captain or chief they'd worked with in the past.

"You'd be hard pressed to beat this story," said Johnny, the firefighter who was more of a listener than a talker. "When I first started with the department, I had a captain who was a nervous guy. He was always prim and proper, wouldn't say 'shit' if his mouth was full of it, and he wasn't the least bit interested in sports. It seemed every time the World Series was on, he'd insist we'd do house inspections.

"It was his turn to do house inspection for fire safety. It was just our luck, the World Series was playing their final game, and of course, he decided we had to do house inspections right at that hour knowing we wanted to watch it. The guys were a little pissed to say the least so decided to play a trick on him.

"One of the guys had a girlfriend who was a bus driver and a big buxom lady, I mean really big and very well-endowed."

At this juncture he made an exaggerated gesture with his hands to the amusement of the coffee drinkers.

"She was also a good sport and full of fun and a willing participant. Her home just happened to be on the inspection list. It was arranged for the captain to inspect her home, while the other three men on the pump with him would inspect adjacent homes in the neighbourhood."

The very thought of it made Johnny laugh. He had to stop telling the story.

"Come on, Johnny, you've just got us all interested," said a guy across the table.

"OK, sorry, as I think about it, I cannot help laughing. You'd had to have known this captain to fully appreciate it. Anyway, he goes to this address, all prim and proper in his meticulous uniform, and rings the doorbell. The big lady answers the door wearing a housecoat. He explains he is from the fire department and wants to inspect her home to check for fire hazards. She invites him in and he walks through the home and she follows. When they get to her bedroom, she whips off her housecoat and is buck naked underneath. She throws him down on the bed and flops on top of him cackling like a banshee and smothering him with her big hooters."

At this point Johnny is laughing so hard it took three tries to get the word hooters out. The men at the table couldn't help but laugh with him; one choked on his coffee.

Johnny managed to continue: "The captain was flabbergasted and being a slight man had to really struggle to get out from under her. Whopper that she was. It scared the holy hell out of him. He ran out the building to the fire engine and put the siren on. And, as you all know, this is the signal for the others to return quickly, so they came running to see what was going on.

"He ordered the driver to go directly to the chief's office, and told the chief he was never *ever* going to do house inspections again. He wanted the chief to call the police but he pacified him, and told him it wasn't necessary. Shortly after the chief issued a directive that read: 'Henceforth all house inspections will be performed as a twosome.'

The men were still laughing when, at the far end of the table, Joe spoke up: "I had a district chief who was unbelievable and I had the dubious honour of being his driver. I haven't heard anything about him for years and wouldn't be surprised if he's dead from a heart attack by now. He was so nervous, always excited and wound up tighter than a seven-day clock. He was a little on the short side with bulging muscles. We referred to him as The Bull.

"I remember one time it was a hot summer afternoon, he'd grabbed the address and we raced out to the car. I had barely shut the door when he banged on the dash shouting, 'Hurry up, laddie! Hurry up, laddie! We've a fire to put out!'

"The car was an older Dodge station wagon and horrible to drive, and scary on turns and corners. Needless to say we were first on the scene, leaving the rescue vehicle a long ways behind. The chief jumped out but forgot to undo his seat belt and was outside the car when it snapped him back in. There was a crowd of people watching this embarrassing performance."

His recollection drew laughter from around the table that could be heard throughout the station.

Joe continued: "He ran into the house through all the smoke and came out with a pot that had been left unattended on the stove. He got to the front steps, dropped the pot of burnt potatoes on the lawn, then fell down on his knees coughing and his face was beetroot red. Can you picture this? A district chief in uniform on his hands and knees, mucus running out of his nose, tears running down his face, gasping for air. It wasn't a pretty sight.

"When the rescue squad went about setting up the fans to clear the smoke, they were all grinning from ear to ear. It seemed to take forever for The Bull to pull himself up by the handrails of the steps and stagger over to the car. He gasped for air and blew his nose all the way back to the station. Not a word was spoken about the incident.

"On another occasion, it was on a hot Sunday afternoon, and The Bull caught the bus to work. He always arrived about an hour earlier than necessary and this day was no different. We kept the overhead doors closed to keep the station cool and the street people out. Across the street was a five-storey hotel where someone had thrown a mattress on fire out of a window.

"The bus The Bull was on came around the corner and he must have seen smoke. So he hurried off the bus, ran across the street and tried to put the fire out by stomping on the mattress. The man on watch in the station announced over the P.A. for everyone to come to the front door to see the spectacle of the District Chief in full uniform, white shirt and cap, dancing on a mattress. The more he danced, the more smoke appeared. He was merely fanning the fire. After much laughter we decided to extinguish it with a couple of pails of water, but the captain stopped us; he was enjoying the chief's performance more than anyone. He finally relented and gave his consent.

"The Bull removed his tunic and cap and finally gave in. As he crossed the street, we all scattered. He came in exhausted, perspiration running in grey streaks down his face and his white shirt was a disaster. The captain came out of his office and shouted for us to go extinguish the fire.

"But the funniest time of all was when he ran through a ravine. I can recall it just as though it was yesterday. We were called out to a garage fire. Again, it was a hot summer day in the afternoon.

"The address was close to the black mud ravine and I inadvertently drove to the wrong side of the damn thing. Black smoke could be seen above the trees. The Bull wouldn't wait to drive around to it. He jumped out the car and went running down the slope. The first tree branch whipped off his hat. I remember running down and picking it up before driving with flashing lights to the other side. There was no stopping The Bull. He was crossing the ravine.

"When I got to the other side, the captain came over and asked, 'Where's the chief?' I told him he should appear shortly, breaking through those trees. I pointed to the ravine.

"We extinguished the fire rather quickly. There was a group of us firefighters waiting for the chief. At last, we could hear him crashing through the woods and then there he was. His tie was twisted to one side, he was beetroot red and totally out of wind. His shirt was torn and there was blood marks on his arms. He collapsed to the ground and someone called for water. Three or four attended to him.

"He finally got up on his knees, drank the water and inquired about the fire. He was assisted to his feet and he shuffled over to the burned out garage, looked at it for a few minutes and then went to the car.

"He scolded me all the way back to the station for driving to the wrong side of the ravine.

"He said, 'When we get back to the station, you better study the map and get to know your district.'

"Upon his request, I never drove him again."

After the long stories about The Bull, Joe's mouth was dry. He went to the stove to pour himself more coffee but the pot was dry too. *Damn it anyway,* he thought.

The men were aptly entertained by Johnny and Joe's narrations but now considered what their new captain would be like. They would surely miss the flamboyant O'Sullivan, despite his aggravating ways; partly for his entertaining qualities, but moreover for his fearlessness on the job. *He* would never be called a *Doorman.* He took the lead up the ladder–often without underwear.

Garth sat at the end of the table totally amused.

Is there no end to the all the pranks? I think not.

Although not present at the table when the men were reminiscing, O'Sullivan also had heard the rumour, so when Chief Watson called him into his office and gave him his transfer papers, he showed no surprise, much to the Watson's disappointment.

I should have known nothing is confidential around this bloody fire hall.

The next day the bulletin board held a memo announcing the transfer of Sean O'Sullivan and the arrival of the new captain, Ivan Whitehall.

Chief Watson was scheduled to give Ivan a private tour of the new station later on during the evening.

***

"Get off your lazy arses and clean up this filthy station!" He sounded like a sergeant major at an army boot camp.

It was the early shift when Captain Whitehall stood in the doorway of the kitchen, his eyes blazing beneath a hank of black hair that had fallen over one eye. He was a big man, standing close to six feet. The tone of his voice matched his demeanour.

"Who the hell's in charge of the bathrooms?"

"That would be me," stated Garth, who stood up, squared his shoulders and walked over to the new captain. Not often was he pleased to be six foot two but he definitely was at this moment.

"I want to see the bathrooms clean, do you hear me, *clean*! I do not want to see any rings in the toilet bowl, yellow stains in the urinal or grime in the sink. I want to see the taps and mirrors shining. I want to see a floor that holds no dirt. I want it clean, spotlessly clean! That includes those bolts at the base of the toilet. Do you understand me?"

Garth was speechless. He'd already cleaned the bathrooms that morning but he wasn't about to tell the captain that. He nodded his head and walked out of the room to begin the task of meeting the new captain's standards.

"I don't know who cleans this kitchen but it's absolutely putrid," said the new captain. "The stove looks like it hasn't been cleaned since this station opened. The window is filthy. The countertops and the floors have layers of gunk and the shelves in the cupboard that hold your mugs–mugs you put your mouth to–look like they haven't been cleaned!"

When he was talking, the men at the table looked around the kitchen with baffled expressions on their faces.

Captain Whitehall pushed the hair off his forehead and wiped the foam from his mouth. He continued in a voice that had grown raspy: "The pool table and television area are a complete mess. There's dust an inch thick every-where. When is the last time a vacuum hit that area? All the windows in this building are dirty–can't see out of them. I want this disaster rectified over the next eight hours, or there will be hell to pay!"

This was the introduction of Captain Whitehall. If they thought O'Sullivan was a pain they had just learned that Whitehall was nothing short of a clean freak soon earning the nick name of Mr. Clean.

They also learned that he was a light sleeper. This was exacerbated by the loud, pig-snorting, rooting-sow sounds of Chief Watson snoring in the officers' quarters where Whitehall had his bunk. In short order, Whitehall moved into the main dorm with the men. He went to bed late and liked to read, but the glow of the light over his bed disturbed the crew who was trying to sleep. This aggravation turned into fodder for the pranksters in the fire station. Things started to happen to Captain Whitehall. All kinds of things.

It was after midnight on the nightshift when Captain Whitehall retired to bed. He sat on the bedside in his blue polka-dot shorts and pulled off one sock, and then the other, grunting with each yank. He was dog-tired but needed to read for a short time to help him get to sleep. He fluffed his pillow, picked up his book and found the mark. Then he pulled back the covers and swung his feet into bed.

His yelp could be heard throughout the station as the springs and mattress crashed to the floor. There was a round of muffled chuckles from the beds of the crew who had purposely feigned slumber–it was a long wait but worth every minute.

That'll fix Mr. Clean Freak, Tidy Bowl!

He ran over to the wall and turned on all the dorm lights.

"Listen up, you bastards, this horseshit has got to stop. I should get everyone of you up washing walls 'til daylight. I've had enough of your crap!"

The cords in his neck were bulging.

Garth, who wasn't privy to the plans of the prank, was quick to give a hand in helping him put the bed back together. Wisely, Captain Whitehall, after gingerly crawling back into bed, decided to put out his light and go to sleep.

The following evening at 6:00 PM, he conducted roll call and read the riot act.

"I am your captain and you *will* have respect for me. Do you understand? If there is anyone here who doesn't understand, speak up now."

The men stood quietly with their heads down, halos shining and angel wings folded.

The days passed by and Captain Whitehall continued with his disruptive behaviour. He would go to bed later than the rest of the men, eventually drifting off to sleep with the light still glowing.

On the last night of the shift before the six days off, Captain Whitehall came to bed late again. He found the mark in his book and settled in for some reading. He turned his light on and pulled up the covers. His light began flashing on and off like a neon sign.

Oh, for fuck's sake!

He got dressed and went back out to the television room, but never said a word.

Chief Watson wasn't surprised to see Captain Whitehall come through his doorway. He had expected him a lot sooner and was anxious to talk to him. He wasn't going to call him in. He felt it prudent to wait for Whitehall to come to him.

"What can I do for you, Ivan?" He smiled and levelled his gaze unwaveringly.

"I think I have the crew ganging up against me," said Ivan. "I'm not sure how to handle it."

"What makes you think that?"

The chief knew exactly what he was going to tell him but was eager to hear Whitehall's version of events.

"Last week when I got into bed, it collapsed."

"So that was the ruckus I heard about midnight."

"Yeah, and last night when I got into bed and wanted to read, someone had put a flashing light in my bed lamp."

"What time did all this happen, Ivan?"

"Oh, about midnight or thereabouts."

"That's awfully late to be going to bed wouldn't you say? Some of those men had been out on a call and needed to sleep. Mighty short-sighted of you."

"What? Are you siding with them? I thought we officers would be sticking together."

"When is the last time you read our mission statement? You need to read it again and then tell me what our main objective is here in the fire hall," said the chief.

"I know what our main objective is. It's to serve the public by being first responders at an accident and get to a fire quickly to put a fire out and to save lives."

"And how do you accomplish that? It's not by banging the men over the head with cleanliness, and by disturbing their sleep at night by keeping your light on!"

"How does that have anything to do with anything?"

"I can tell you haven't been a captain very long, Ivan. If you'd had, you'd know harmony and cooperation is the most vital thing on any job, especially when fighting a fire or attending an accident scene. Just think about it for a minute, man. Yes, we need to keep the fire station clean, I concur. But there's an easier and more beneficial way–not by bullying. I know you've heard that old cliché: 'You can catch more flies with honey than with vinegar.' You've been here only a short while and already you've gone through gallons of vinegar. Try some honey for a change and you'll see a big difference."

Captain Whitehall sat speechless with his head down, listening intently.

Perhaps I should change my ways, perhaps I've been too hard on the men. I'll be different from now on but it's not going to be easy.

The next evening Garth participated in a department hockey game and to his dismay, he noticed Hawks was also on the ice playing for the opposition. Hawks had control of the puck on a breakaway. Garth, after him caught him just inside the blue line and took the puck away, then skated around the net. As he came alongside, Hawks put out his stick to purposely trip him, and then skated away. Garth hit the ice hard but he didn't stay down long. He was up on his skates and after Hawks who had turned to face his wrath. With both hands on his stick, Garth held it horizontally and cross-checked Hawks and sent him sprawling. "That'll teach you for tripping me, you son of a bitch."

Hawks got up slowly. Both men took off their gloves and the punching began. Hawks managed a clean punch to Garth's nose and blood spurted. At the sight of this, Garth threw all caution to the wind and was bent on flattening him. He saw his opening and raised his fist, but the deadly punch was stopped in midair by the referee.

"Knock it off! There's to be no fighting in our games. What the hell's the matter with you two jackasses? Now get back in the game or go home. It's your choice."

Garth with an ashen and bloodied face began to explain but the referee stopped him.

"I don't want to hear any of that—just take your choice: out or in."

Garth wiped his face on a cloth the ref had handed him and skated back onto the ice to join his team members. Hawks, on the other hand, skated into the dressing room to change and go home.

CHAPTER

13

AFTER AN EVENING WITH KYLA, GARTH WOULD always wake up the next morning feeling elated. Their relationship was becoming stronger with every date—last evening was no exception. He discovered they both shared the same sense of humour and always spent an enjoyable time together.

Today he was starting the early shift and as planned there would be a breakfast cooked by a rookie firefighter called Lance. He had been bragging about his cooking expertise, so today he was going to put his money where his mouth was and cook breakfast.

Lance was just coming in with the groceries when Garth arrived at the station. Before heading into the kitchen he collected everyone's share of the cost. They were sitting in the lounge waiting to be summoned to breakfast.

"I'm starving this morning," said Charlie. "We've a big training day ahead of us."

"I'm going to need my *groceries* this morning. It's always a good idea to start off the day with a hearty breakfast," stated Garth, who was in fact, quoting Kyla. He often referred to his meals as his groceries, which always made everyone smile.

"Breakfast is served!" exclaimed Lance in a singsong tone of announcement. The hungry firefighters were instantly on their feet and made their way into the kitchen.

Garth couldn't believe his eyes. On top of the stove were four frying pans, each one half-full of bubbling oil. Bacon, sausages, sliced potatoes and fried eggs were bouncing in it. Oil was spitting all over the stove. He'd never seen so much oil on food before and he wondered how he could possibly eat it. He was thankful to see a large platter of unbuttered toast in the middle of the table, which proved to be some consolation. He was also able to sponge some of his food with a paper towel, as did the others. The men got through the meal counterbalanced with the toast then headed to the training centre.

Captain Whitehall called Lance aside.

"The guys could barely eat your breakfast. Whatever possessed you to cook with so much oil?"

"I wanted to make it taste good."

"What you served was beyond overkill. One tablespoon would have been enough, not two cups."

"I'll do better next time."

Reflecting on his conversation with Chief Watson, he said, "Fair enough, now let's head over to the training centre."

After radioing the call centre to say Station 5 would not be receiving calls, Chief Watson requested Garth Winters be his driver for the short journey to the training station.

The chief prided himself in how well-trained his platoon was and he intended to keep it that way by frequent training sessions. Those sessions would last most of the day on how to stabilize at an accident scene, perform extrication, resuscitation, and the method on how to stop blood flow while waiting for the ambulance. After a fire or accident, they sat around the table critiquing their actions, while constantly striving toward improvement.

Today they would drive one mile to the other end of the property to the training station and practice laying of lines, using the aerial and pump, and examining the functionality of all the auxiliary apparatus in both the aerial and rescue units.

Time would also be spent in the smoke house with its sliding walls in the six-floor training tower, which simulated a high-rise building when aerial ladders were needed. As always, the emphasis was placed on finding and saving victims.

Garth would be reminded of the incident with Hawks, each time he frequented the training centre. He had expected to run into him on a regular basis but had only seen him once seated at a nearby table at the calendar dance. At that time, he noticed him staring at Kyla when she was dancing. *The coyote!*

As time passed by, the horror of the incident was diminishing. He could now be in this place without dread.

The last session of the day was designated to using the aerial. While a reinforcement lesson was beneficial to everyone, it was Lance, the bad-cook rookie, who needed it most. An explanation on how the ladder operated was given by Captain Whitehall. Both he and Lance stood at the base of the aerial atop the apparatus. He demonstrated how the ladder was to be extended one segment at a time, carrying the hose with it and how at this point, the aerial traversed the pump at a forty-five degree angle.

As Captain Whitehall tried to manipulate the switches at the base, he realized the nozzle at the end of the ladder was stuck. He turned to Lance and said, "Here, take this hammer and go up and see if you can loosen it."

Lance, though fearful, followed his command and climbed up the angled ladder. As he neared the top, the ladder bent down toward the ground, tipping the truck up sideways by two feet.

"Drop the hammer and hang on! Hang on!"

The men could see what was about to happen and shouted up to him from the ground. Before Lance could react, the truck righted itself, snapping the ladder back with such rebounding force he screamed as he was catapulted thirty feet to the ground. He landed with a sickening thud.

"Oh, no!" exclaimed the captain as he and the men hurried to Lance's side.

Amidst the panic, Chief Watson hollered, "Damn it, damn it!" while telling himself, *Stay calm, stay calm!*

Garth was first at his side. "Don't move, Lance, we'll take care of you." The fully conscious man moaned and tried to get up. "Please stay still. You *must* stay still, Lance."

Chief Watson had run to the radio in the cab and ordered an ambulance but Garth intervened: "I can have him to the hospital before the ambulance leaves the parking lot. He's bound to have internal bleeding. Let's get him on a stretcher and into the rescue unit *right now*. I need several men to carefully support every part of his body when we move him."

The authority in Garth's voice moved the men quickly. Within seconds their siren was blaring down the street towards the hospital. Chief Watson had radioed ahead to the hospital and as they pulled up to the door of the ER, the emergency staff came out with a stretcher to meet them. They immediately whisked him away to the operating room.

The men sat in the waiting room waiting for the prognosis. Faced with the first in-house catastrophe of his career, Chief Watson was clearly upset. Captain Whitehall, whose face was ashen and overwrought with guilt for sending him up the ladder, kept repeating, "I didn't see it coming, I just didn't see it coming."

Garth replayed the accident over and over again in his mind. He was trying to think of a way it could have and should have been prevented.

An hour later, the doctor came out and gave his report: "He's been stabilized. It's a good thing you brought him down when you did. Any time later might have been too late. We've completed an abdominal X-ray and operated to stop the internal bleeding. More X-rays are needed to evaluate what bones have been broken. We strongly suspect his neck is broken. However, until we have more information, we will do all we can to prevent total paralysis. Right now he is heavily sedated and sleeping and will need to rest."

"When can I see him?" asked Chief Watson.

"Not for a couple of days. We are keeping him sedated."

Sorrow filled Station No. 5 as the news spread that one of their own was injured. The coffee room was quiet. There was no one playing pool and no one watched television. Most of the men stayed in their rooms reading or just sitting quietly.

District Chief Watson asked everyone to meet with him first thing in the morning then he left to visit Lance's wife. He asked Garth to join him.

At first when Watson told Lance's wife that his neck might have been broken, she was filled with disbelief and then absolute sorrow. She covered her face and began to cry. "He must be in so much pain, poor darling."

Through her tears she said, "Now that he had steady work, we were planning to start a family."

Garth was first to respond and placed his arm around her shoulder. "He may still be alright. The doctors are doing all they can for him."

"How did a thing like this happen?" she sobbed.

"Just a freak accident. These things happen in all walks of life. One just never knows when an accident might happen," explained Garth. *Freak accident, hmm!* He was thinking about all the questions he was going to ask and hoped for answers.

The chief watched in admiration at how Garth offered his consolation and took hold of the situation.

"Have you got someone to call to stay with you and go with you to the hospital?" asked Garth.

"I'll call my sister. She lives next door." She picked up the phone.

"Linda," she sobbed, "can you come over right away. Something has happened to Lance."

Within a few moments, the front door opened and her sister walked in. The firemen watched as the two women embraced, and then left to make their way back to the station.

Chief Hadley had been informed of the accident and called an emergency meeting. "Are we all here?" he asked.

Chief Watson looked around and then nodded, "Yes, Sir."

"I would like you all to write one short paragraph relating to what happened today, and then I want you to list three things you think could have been done to avoid it. Keep it short and to the point."

He turned to Chief Watson and said, "Put them on my desk."

He walked out the room with his head down, filled with apprehension of what lay ahead. He knew there'd be inquiries and even an inquest by one or more authorities on a day that would live in his memory forever.

Garth had gathered up the papers, as requested, and was laying them on the captain's desk when a call came in: "Apartment fire Third Street."

In an instant the men had cleared the fire station and were speeding down the street, siren and air horn clearing their path. When they arrived at the scene, they were quick to note it was a three-alarm. Station 2 and 3 were already there.

The six-storey building had smoke billowing from most of the top level, and it appeared there was more smoke halfway down and again on the lower level. This was going to be a tricky one. Lines were laid, aerials were raised and firefighters were in action. There were several ambulances parked out front with medical attendants working feverishly with victims.

A firefighter was bringing a lady down covered with a blanket to shield her from the cold. Two-thirds down he shouted to Garth who was first on the scene from Station 5: "Look after this one. I have to go back up, there are more victims."

Garth moved forward and assisted the lady who was moaning, "I'm having a baby,"

"We better get you to the hospital right away," said Garth.

His heart picked up a beat as he moved towards the waiting ambulance. The attendants placed her on a gurney, which they hoisted up into the back of the ambulance. Just then another person, who was unconscious, was brought down the ladder. The ambulance attendants diverted their attention to this new victim and began working on him, leaving Garth on his own with the expectant mother. She lay writhing on the gurney, and for the second time in the past twenty-four hours, Garth found that he was giving words of consolation.

"Just hang in there, ma'am. We'll have you to the hospital soon." He spoke to her from the open door of the ambulance.

"Soon!" she screamed. "Soon isn't good enough. The baby is coming now. Now! Do you hear me? Now! Oh, my God, it's coming!"

Garth stepped into the ambulance and shut the door saying, "Oh dear!" He was in unfamiliar territory. All he could do was draw from the smidgen amount of training he'd received about delivering babies when training as a fire-fighter several months ago.

With trembling hands he pulled the covers back and pulled off the wet, panties. He reached for a towel from a nearby shelf and spread it under the lady's bottom. Her pubic hair was matted down as fluid gushed from her. He could see the vagina opening and something beginning to protrude. He fought to control the nausea that was constricting his throat. The lady gave an ear-bending scream and a long guttural grunt and the infant slithered out into his hands. He reached for another towel and almost dropped the wet, slippery baby.

Oh, oh! What to do now? Must keep this baby warm, must get it crying!

The thought no sooner raced across his mind when the new little piece of humanity began to cry and to shiver. He shouted, "You have a son!" then grabbed more towels and wrapped the baby with just a little peephole for it to breathe at one end, and another at the other end for the umbilical cord, which was still attached to the mother and then lay the baby on her chest.

"Thank you, thank you!" she whimpered. Garth wiped his hands on a towel and took off his bunker coat and put it on top of the blanket, carefully covering both mother and child.

Within minutes of the baby being born, the medic opened the door. His eyes widened at the firefighter sitting there shivering with only his undershirt on beneath his suspenders.

"What are you doing without your coat?" he asked.

"Just covering the lady and her baby. I didn't see any more blankets in here."

"Baby?" he queried. "Did you say baby?"

"Yup, just delivered it a few moments ago. It's still attached to the mother. We better get them to the hospital."

The medic reached for a couple of blankets in a drawer at the side of the ambulance.

"Here," he said. "Wrap up in this and put one over the lady and stay with her, and we'll get her off to the hospital. More medics are on scene to take care of those out there. This has been one hell of a fire, and one hell of a day."

"Thanks, I didn't know they were there," said Garth.

The siren blared through the streets as the ambulance raced to the hospital. In the back lay a mother and her newborn cloaked in yellow bunker gear. Guarding them sat a firefighter draped in a grey, Hudson's Bay woollen blanket thinking, *I can't believe it. I've just delivered a baby. Wow! Kyla will find this amusing.*

CHAPTER

14

A DARK CLOUD HUNG OVER FIRE STATION NO. 5 IN Papillon, Saskatchewan, like fog over the grasslands. It had been many years since there had been an accident at the station, and the men were mournful over an incident that had put their colleague in hospital. The feeling of guilt amongst the men was intense; in particular District Chief Watson, who sat at his desk in a state of depression knowing that he was the man in charge, and ultimately where the buck stopped.

He recalled the day of the accident and how he had considered whether or not to cancel the training session beforehand. However, rookies needed training, and the regular men needed review. *Damn it*, he thought, *I should have cancelled the training session for another day.* His thoughts lingered but he knew deep down that it would have made no difference.

All these excuses and what if's don't fix Lance.

He brought his hand across his cheek in despair.

His pang of guilt was interrupted by Chief Hadley, who walked into his office unannounced, pulled up a chair and planted himself in front of his desk.

"You were very quiet at the hearing last night. I expected you would have had more to say under the circumstances."

"What could I say? Captain Whitehall said it all. Nothing I would have said would have changed things. A man is seriously hurt under my watch."

"You might have said, 'I'll make sure it doesn't happen again.'"

"Of course, that is a given."

"What is a given to you isn't necessarily a given to the men at the meeting. I think they would have liked to hear you say it."

"You're right, I should have," replied Watson with his head down.

"This will make the rates paid to Workers' Compensation increase, of course, and therefore our portion of the city's budget," stated Hadley. "Just so I have it right, explain again what went wrong with the stabilizers."

"When we started the training, the stabilizers were released and extended from beneath the truck. Everything appeared to be normal. However, after the accident happened, I noticed the pin, that secures the leg of the stabilizer in place, had broken and snapped off, causing the leg to buckle down. I'm assuming this happened at point of impact. Nothing we could have done would have prevented the accident."

"That is precisely why you mustn't beat yourself up over this. You can't own it. I am suggesting henceforth the pins be replaced on a regular basis. Also, the manufacturer needs to be advised the metallurgical strength of their pins need improvement. I'll be calling them today."

"Thanks, Chief, but I cannot stop feeling badly for our rookie Lance."

"What is his condition? Have you any word on that?"

"We do know now that his neck is broken and it is going to be a long haul for him; more surgeries, a lot of physiotherapy and rehabilitation."

"What is being done about his livelihood? I'm sure your union will have input."

"Oh, yes, they have already," replied Watson. "And like previous accidents that have occurred at other stations, Lance will continue receiving his pay. Eventually he will be employed in the call centre."

Chief Hadley nodded his approval and said, "That's the best that can be done for him. Now, if I'm going to call the pin supplier, I best be going. Keep your chin up and remember accidents do happen. That's why they're called accidents."

He walked out of Watson's office as quickly as he walked in, taking with him some of the angst Watson was feeling.

***

Nightshift had begun with idle firefighters sitting around glumly, drinking coffee and chatting quietly. With time on their hands, they waited patiently for an emergency call that would inevitably summon them into action. Pranks had ceased since the incident with the rookie, and given his current physical state, it would take the men some time before they regained their sense of humour.

Yet, despite the monotony that existed around them at this time, they weren't prepared for the drama that was about to unfold. No one could have possibly known or even guessed this evening was going to have a life-changing effect on one kindhearted firefighter and a warning to all the rest.

The evening moved slowly on and the clock struck 11:00 PM. Still no calls to disturb the tranquil mood, but someone did come to the door: a scantily dressed, teenage girl with long golden hair, shivering and sobbing. When the man in the Watch Box let her in. He was shocked to see someone so young out so late. He escorted her to the kitchen and then quickly returned to man his station.

Working on nightshift was Oscar Price, who was partnered with Garth Winters. He had been contemplating going to bed when the girl was brought to him in the kitchen. She appeared to be the same age as his own daughter and the very thought that she would be out alone at this time of night alarmed him.

The girl was shivering from the cold and wearing only a halter top and shorts. Oscar pulled up a chair and invited her to sit down.

"Can I make you a cup of coffee?" he asked.

"Thank you," she replied gratefully.

"Cream and sugar?" he asked.

"P-p-please," she stammered.

He placed a cup before her, well-laced with sugar and cream. She commenced sipping immediately like she hadn't drunk anything for a week.

Oscar sat across from her at the table, studying her and thinking how pretty she was; long golden, curly hair, she had a round face and the clearest blue eyes he'd seen in a long time.

She'll be a beautiful woman someday!

"Now, I want you to tell me your name and how old you are?" he asked.

She looked up at him and was hesitant to answer, almost as if she was planning a lie she couldn't formulate. "My name is Amanda Wakefield and I'm fifteen years old," she uttered convincingly.

"Do your parents know you're out?" he asked.

"No," she replied. "No, they don't. They don't let me go anywhere. I snuck out to go to my boyfriend's house. He wasn't around and I missed the last bus to get back home and now . . . now I'm in big trouble. My dad is going to kill me for sure."

A fresh round of tears began to roll down her cheeks. He passed a box of tissues to her.

"Where do you live?"

"At the other side of town by the old peanut warehouse that burned down. I don't know how I'm going to get home. I don't know *what* I'm going to tell my dad."

"The truth is the best answer, always," said Oscar, knowing that would have been exactly what he'd tell his own daughter.

"But he's going to freak out, and my mother would have too, if she hadn't died last year. He must have noticed I'm missing. He's probably freaking out right now. I'm in so much trouble," she said, covering her face with her hands.

"I think you should give your father a call. Here's the phone." He handed her the telephone but she refused it.

"No, no, I can't call him! I can't!" She sounded terrified. Oscar felt sorry for her, especially given she'd lost her mother.

"Well, we're going to have to get you home right away. I need to go talk to the captain and tell him I'm leaving. I'll be back in a minute."

He passed through the lounge and spoke to Garth who, along with others, was watching the news, while two firefighters were challenging each other at the pool table.

"Keep an eye on that girl out there. I'm going to see the captain to tell him I'm driving her home. She just appeared at the door."

"Sure," replied Garth, so engrossed in the news he answered without looking at him.

Oscar knocked on the door of the captain's dorm, waking him up. He eventually opened the door dressed in his robe.

"What's up, Oscar?"

"A young girl has come to the station. She needs a ride home and has missed the last bus."

"Call a cab for her," he replied.

"That'll cost the department a lot of money. She lives at the other side of town by that old peanut warehouse. I could run her home."

"You better make it quick. A call could come in and we'd need you on the pump. Let me know when you get back," said the captain as he yawned.

Oscar returned to the kitchen with a report pad and pen. He took down her name and address and noted the time. He went back into the lounge and told Garth where he was headed.

"I should be back within the hour," he said.

"I'll be up," replied Garth.

With his jacket over Amanda's shoulders, he led her out of the station to his car for the drive across town.

The drive was silent. An attempt to make conversation with Amanda was futile. It was as though she was in a completely different world. When approaching her district, she sat on the edge of the seat looking very anxious indeed and she trembled when they pulled up in front of her home. It was a small, white frame house, tidy in appearance.

When Oscar pulled into the driveway, he noticed a man at the window. He came to the front door and Amanda had barely stepped out of the car, when Oscar heard him shout, "Where have you been, young lady?"

Amanda walked slowly and heavy-footed up the sidewalk and her father came down the steps to meet her. He grabbed her by the arm and hauled her up the steps into the house and then slammed the door. This all happened before Oscar could get out of the car and explain why she was with him. He sat in the driveway for a few moments debating whether he should go in and explain, but then considered his absence from the station would leave them short, so he put his car in reverse and headed back.

Amanda was crying uncontrollably as her father berated her. On and on he went without giving her a chance to explain. When he was finally done talking, she screamed, "But Daddy, that firefighter molested me! He took me down a dark road and was so strong, I couldn't fight him! That's why I'm so late." Her sobbing was real.

"He did what?" He was angry, and had heard all he needed to hear from his young daughter. He didn't hesitate to call the police.

Back at the station the team of firefighters sat around aimlessly waiting for their colleague to return. Forty-five minutes later, there was a loud knock on the door. Garth stood up, stretched, and then made his way to the door.

Two city policemen stood tall and erect at the entrance. They introduced themselves as Sergeant O'Malley and Constable Jones from the Papillon Police Department. They wore black uniforms with gold buttons and a city crest on the sleeve. A single yellow stripe ran down the outside of their trousers, which added to their commanding appearance.

"Did any firefighter from this station drive a young lady home tonight?" asked Constable Jones.

"Yes," said Garth. "Oscar Price did. Come on in. I hope he wasn't in a car accident?"

Without further comment, they stepped inside, Garth leading the way into the kitchen. Seeing policemen on the premises grabbed the attention and curiosity of the other men. They sauntered into the kitchen and milled about.

"We would like to speak to Mr. Price, please," said Sergeant O'Malley.

"He hasn't returned," said Garth. "He had a substantial distance to drive. I understand it was clear across town although he should be back very soon."

"We'll wait for him," said the Sergeant.

Garth was about to offer them a cup of coffee when the door opened and to the men's surprise, the union president came in, followed by Chief Hadley.

Something has happened, something serious, thought Garth

"Let's not stand here, let's go into the kitchen and sit down," said Chief Hadley. He and the union president looked devastated as they sat down at the table. Along with the policemen, it was obvious that they were privy to what was going on, while the crowd around the table were anxiously waiting to know. Captain Whitehall attempted to put an end to the mystery.

"What the hell is going on here?" he asked in an exasperated tone.

"You'll find out when Oscar Price returns," the chief replied.

Stilted, small talk commenced around the table; from the weather, their latest fire, as to who won the last hockey game. While it seemed like a long time, it was only minutes when they heard the door open.

Oscar was surprised to see so many people in the kitchen. However, the sight of Chief Hadley, the union president and the police, unnerved him more so.

"What's going on?" he asked.

The two policemen stood up, as did the chief and union president.

"Are you Oscar Price?" the Sergeant asked.

"Yes, I am. Why?"

"Did you drive a young lady by the name of Amanda Wakefield home tonight?" asked Sergeant O'Malley.

"Yes, I did. I delivered her to her father. I'm just getting back now. Why do you ask?"

"Miss Wakefield has stated she was molested by the firefighter that drove her home. We have to take you down to the station for questioning."

Oscar turned as white as snow and could barely speak. "That's a boldface lie if ever there was one! I did no such thing!" His eyes were blazing.

"We have to take you down to the station immediately for questioning. It's a matter of procedure."

They walked out the door leaving behind a room full of shocked firefighters, all of whom would swear on their mother's grave that Oscar would never do such a thing. Chief Hadley and the union president followed them out. They stood for some time talking before the policemen finally drove away.

Garth went to bed but it was several hours before he went to sleep. He knew this story wouldn't be over for some time. All he could do was hope for a swift and successful ending for Oscar.

Oscar would never forget the echoing sound of the lock on his door when the key was turned. He was placed in a cell smelling like metal and disinfectant, and as he looked around at the small space, one sweep of his eyes took in the contents: a hard bunk with its ugly grey blanket, a urinal and toilet, and one wooden chair. He couldn't believe he was charged with molestation and had been arrested. *Will I wake up to discover that this has been nothing more than a bad dream?* he wondered.

How could one small girl have such power to do this terrible thing to him when he was merely looking out for her safety?

He lay down on the bunk and thought of his wife. He would have to phone her in the morning and give her the bad news and she would have to tell the children. They would never understand. They would miss their father and be asking for him. The other members of his family; his parents, brothers and sisters would have to be told. They would be shocked beyond measure.

How could one small girl have such power? he reiterated to himself.

All these thoughts and more entered his mind for most of the night. When sleep finally came the nightmare continued with a dream of being incarcerated for years. He awoke exhausted with a blazing headache and facing two visitors.

Union lawyer Richard Lambert and Chief Hadley stood next to his bed. Oscar sat up. The warden brought in another chair so they could all sit down. Clearly, there was going to be a conversation.

Richard Lambert, a tall man with kind eyes, spoke first: "There will be a bail hearing this morning and the union is prepared to cover it."

"Before we go any further," said Oscar, "please understand one very important fact. I did not touch that girl. I drove her home because she had no other way of getting there. I did not touch her!"

"I believe and support you," said Richard.

In Oscar's tragic world, those words provided a small measure of comfort.

Chief Hadley cleared his throat. "I'm sorry, Oscar, but I cannot say the same. I'm afraid I have to release you from the fire department."

"You mean I'm losing my job over this even though I've done nothing wrong."

"I'm afraid so. I have no alternative. I have the reputation of the department and all other firefighters to think of."

Oscar pounded his fist on his knee and then jumped up.

"It's not fair. It simply isn't fair. All I was doing was trying to get the girl home safely and this is the thanks I get. I'm guilty simply because someone accused me?" His voice was trembling.

Before he had finished speaking, Chief Hadley was out the door, his footsteps loud as he walked down the hall. Richard stood up quickly, stepped forward and put his hand on Oscar's shoulder. "I want you to know, Oscar, that we will be investigating every possible aspect of this charge. Rest assured, no stone will be left unturned. I have to leave now and prepare for the bail hearing. I'll see you in the courtroom." His voice was ringing with sincerity.

**

Oscar stood before the judge with Richard Lambert at his side while the charges were read:

"Oscar Price, you are charged with molesting Amanda Wakefield on July 31st, 1969. How do you plead?"

"Absolutely, not guilty, your honour."

Richard spoke next. "Your Honour, I am requesting bail be set for Mr. Price. He is a family man and is needed in his home."

"The bail is set at five thousand dollars," said the judge as he brought the gavel down.

"Thank you," said Richard.

In attendance, the union president went to the desk and wrote out the cheque. Oscar shook their hands and left with his lawyer to return to the fire station to collect his things and drive home.

The firefighters on duty gave their condolences and support. They all declared they knew he was innocent and that it was unfair that he was fired. "You'll be cleared," they had said unanimously. Oscar drove away without being able to look back.

Richard Lambert pulled up a chair and sat with the men at Station 5. He was offered a coffee but refused cream and sugar. "I take coffee just like my whiskey, straight up. Actually, I'm here to investigate what happened last night with Oscar Price. I want you guys to tell me everything you know about Oscar and anything, anything at all, you know about what went down."

Comments flew around the table like a flock of squawking magpies:

"It's a bunch of bullshit. I don't know how that little wench can get away with it!"

"How can the chief fire someone without evidence?"

"I don't have any respect for Hadley! He should be locked up!"

"We should all walk off the job."

"Oscar would never do anything like that. Hell, he's got a daughter the same age."

"What proof do they have? Actually, none!"

"It will never go to trial, I just know it!"

"If this is the kind of boss we have, hell, why should we put our lives on the line?"

"Just a minute, fellas," said Lambert, "I know how you all must feel. I agree with everything you've said. But now I must try to make some legal sense of it. I realize those on nights will have gone home, however, I need to know who was working last night?

"Was there a report filled out, like the time Oscar left and where he was going, and what time he returned?"

"Of course, we make reports on everything we do."

"Could I please get a copy of it?"

"I passed Garth Winters in the parking lot this morning when he was going home," said the firefighter at the head of the table. "I'm sure he would be more than happy to talk to you. I can get his number for you and a copy of the report."

"Thanks, that would be great."

Richard Lambert didn't waste any time calling Garth. They agreed to meet at Jerry's Coffee House on Second Street for coffee.

"Oscar asked me to keep an eye on her when he'd left the room to tell the captain he was driving her home. The little cockroach just sat at the table drinking a cup of coffee. It was likely that she had already planned how she was going to frame him," stated Garth.

"I have the report here," said Richard, reaching into his briefcase. "It shows they left at 11:30 PM to drive to her home, which is at the other side of town. It doesn't say on the report what time he returned. That space is blank on the report."

"I'm not surprised. The place was buzzing with police and bigwigs last night. Oscar wouldn't have been in any frame of mind to stop and fill that in."

"Then we have no idea how long he was gone, do we?"

"Oh, yes we do," declared Garth. "I looked at my watch when he came in. It was exactly 12:40 AM."

"Next we need to know how long that drive would have taken him. I should take a run out there to see. I have the address here," said Richard, pointing at the report.

"Why don't we do the drive tonight at the exact same time?' said Garth, "The traffic is always different in the evening. I'm on days off so have the time."

"Good idea," said Richard. "I'll meet you at Station 5 tonight at 11:15 PM."

"You got it," replied Garth excited about the possibility of getting Oscar freed from this catastrophe.

At precisely 11.30 PM Garth and Richard drove out from the station to the Price home, turned around, and then drove back. They returned at 12:38 AM. It took them one hour and eight minutes. Oscar's trip took one hour and ten minutes, only two minutes longer, and hardly enough time to drive down a lonely road and molest a young girl. Amanda Wakefield was lying–no question about it!

Richard knew exactly what he had to do next. He took his report to the prosecutor's office and showed him the results, who in turn visited the police department.

It took two more weeks before all charges against Oscar Price were dropped. When cornered, Amanda admitted that her story was fabricated; she was referred to a Juvenile Court.

It was the longest two weeks of Oscar's life. He was surprised to see Chief Hadley on his doorstep the next day. The Chief apologized profusely and gave him his job back and all of his lost wages. But no price could be put on the anguish he had suffered. The chief's reputation as a leader who didn't respect his firefighters would follow him for very long time.

One week later, he sent the following directive:

URGENT TO ALL FIREFIGHTERS IN THE CITY OF PAPILLON

Recently one of our firefighters was accused of molestation after driving a young female home.

Before it went to court, she recanted and said she made it up to get attention from her father. Needless to say the firefighter suffered immeasurably when he thought he was only doing her a favour. A possible bad reflection on the Papillon Fire Department was averted.

If at any time, in the future, someone comes to your station–especially a female–needing a ride home, under no circumstances will you provide the transportation. If this occurs, you will call the local police department and place it in their hands.

There will be no exception.

Chief G. Hadley

CHAPTER

15

FIRE STATION NO. 5 WAS INCIDENT-FREE FOR SEVERAL days and the firefighters sat around the table waiting for dinner to be served by Oscar Price, the self-acclaimed chef. He was preparing his famous fish and chips dinner and had just spent considerable time peeling potatoes, cutting them into thick strips and rinsing them to remove the excess starch. Three bottles of ketchup were placed on the table along with a large salt shaker and a plate of lemon wedges. They were going to have a feast!

The halibut fillets lay on a large platter all ready for dipping in the batter, which he said was a secret recipe. A large pan of oil was heating on the stove. He had a dish towel in his hand and a smile on his face, anticipating compliments from the hungry men when the atmosphere was rudely interrupted by a call, which was loud and clear:

"Residence fire at 5536 Norton Road."

The firefighters responded with immediate effect and jumped in their bunker gear and were out the door in less than a minute. As they climbed the hill to reach the address at the north end of the city, they could see smoke streaming out the front door and flowing across and down the street. All of the high-end, large homes were built in close proximity, making a fire a challenge to contain.

Most of the residents were out on the street. They had to step aside for the big trucks that were arriving to deliver timber, for yet another big home under that was under construction.

The widow who lived at 5536 was crying and kept repeating over and over again, "I don't know how this could have happened. I want my children's pictures."

"It's not safe for you to go back in," she was told by one of the men. The firefighters were entering with a line. "Is there anyone in the home?" she was asked.

"No, I live alone," she sobbed. "My gentleman friend was here earlier but he left to play Texas Hold'em. If he'd stayed, I know he would've put the fire out right away. He used to be a firefighter, you know, one of the best!" She dabbed her eyes with a tissue.

They discovered the fire was burning in the basement and had originated from a floor heater in one of the bedrooms. The heater shorted creating a fire on the carpet. It swiftly spread to some pillows stored nearby. The firefighters extinguished it thereby averting a total disaster. The damage to the lower level of the widow's home was minimal.

They spent considerable time at the residence making certain the fire was totally extinguished. The widow offered them coffee and donuts. They were mighty hungry not having had their special fish and chips dinner. She thanked them for their great effort and for saving her home.

As they were driving back to the station, a call came over the radio:

"Station 8 has strung a line into station 5."

What! There's a fire at our station! They turned on the siren and put the pedal to the metal all the way back, weaving in and out of traffic, almost rear-ending some cars on the way.

Oscar feared the worst. He thought it must have been the oil boiling for the fish and chip dinner. He couldn't remember turning off the stove. He did remember flinging the dish towel on the counter near the stove, but from there he drew a blank.

Oh no! It must be my fault!

His heart was racing.

The sight of smoke caught their attention as they pulled up at Station No. 5, right on the heels of the crew from Station No. 8.

"It's in the kitchen!" one shouted.

Oh no, thought Oscar.

"Check the bunks! Make sure the station's clear," shouted another.

After an hour, the building was declared safe but the wet and smoked-up kitchen was totally burnt out.

No one could have felt worse than Oscar. This wasn't his year; the accusation by the teenage girl and now this. Would he ever be able to live this down? It didn't take long for the blame to be laid on his doorstep.

A few days later, Captain Whitehall stopped Oscar in the parking lot. "Chief Hadley would like to see you as soon as possible," he said.

What will my punishment be? Will I be fired?

These thoughts and others travelled across his mind. When the chief interviewed him about the incident, all Oscar could say was, "It was my fault. I'm sorry."

"It's not so long ago that I was saying sorry to you, Oscar," said the chief. "This evens the score, wouldn't you say? We will forget about this incident and can only hope it never happens again."

"Thank you," replied Oscar. "It won't happen again."

The emotional scars Oscar was left with by his unjust arrest and subsequent firing were finally wiped away.

A kitchen table was set up in the apparatus room, and a hot plate was placed on another small table with the coffee supplies. The firefighters had to sit next to the big pumps for their coffee and meals while the kitchen was repaired. The disgruntled men were not short of words, expressing their displeasure at settling for one-pot dinners.

They used the time, however, to tell stories of some of the firefighters' infamous pranks. Laughter filled the apparatus room as each related an episode, as though in competition with one another for the funniest tale.

"We had a visit from a firefighter from another station to attend one of our critique sessions. He was a Mister Perfect type of guy, always groomed to the nines. We snuck out and put black shoe polish on the underside of his steering wheel and on the handle of the air brakes. Needless to say his hands wouldn't be so lily white when he got back to his station."

"We did something similar but instead we put it on the inside front of the hat. It was a hot day and when he took his hat off he had an ugly, black mark across his forehead."

"Here's a good one. We put a sock in the soup pot. Can you imagine how shocked the next person who went to fill their bowl would have been?"

"I hope it was a clean sock!"

"We would put red food colouring in the mashed potatoes, and also separated Oreo cookies, scooped out the icing and filled them with toothpaste."

"We would fill one of the coffee cups with water and place it on the second shelf. When someone reached for it, he would get a face full of water."

"Listen to this one—syrup on the floor outside the shower so it would be stepped in and have to rewash their feet?"

"This guy at my last station bought a new car and was told it would get excellent mileage. He was so proud of that fact. Well, we got together and decided we would play a little trick on him. We filled a can with gas and each day secretly added more into his tank. He would come into the kitchen with his little mileage book with records he kept like the Holy Grail, and brag about how great his new car was doing. Then we stopped adding the gas and began syphoning. The poor bugger was shocked how his car was guzzling the petrol. He checked it for days and became despondent, but before he took it back to the dealer we fessed up."

"One of our captains held a house party at his home. On his front lawn was a large ornament of a pig. His girlfriend had painted the toenails of this damn pig a bright red. It was the stupidest looking thing I have ever seen. The next morning when the captain got up, it was gone–someone had stolen it. Then the ransom notes started happening: 'I've got your pig', 'good luck trying to find it.' As many as fifteen ransom notes were sent but he couldn't find out who had it. The men felt sorry for him so delivered a real live pig to his home—about two months old. Its toenails were painted red with the captain's name written on its back."

"A lady firefighter—actually she was the first one at this particular station—had been given a hard time by the men, so she decided to get even. She baked a chocolate cake; a nice tall one, iced to perfection. Smiling, she offered everyone a generous slab with their coffee. This wasn't any ordinary chocolate cake. It was laced with copious amounts of Exlax. I don't have to tell you guys what happened next."

The storyteller's laughter rippled up from his toes.

These were the stories told around the table in the apparatus room—amusement for the men while they waited for a call and their new kitchen.

When Oscar came in to join them, he poured himself a coffee and sat down.

"Well if it isn't Smokey," someone declared, which drew a fresh round of laughter.

Garth thought, *Oh, Oh, here we go again.*

Oscar knew his new name would last forever and after all he had been through, he didn't care one leaping little lick.

CHAPTER

16

DON SYMINGTON, CITY ADMINISTRATOR FOR PAPILLON held this position for nigh on thirty years. He walked across the parking lot of City Hall towards his automobile. He was deep in thought, and he was worried. He was on his way to visit Chief George Hadley. The fact George pulled a few strings to employ his son at Station No. 5 in replacement of the firefighter who'd fallen off the ladder, complicated things immensely.

In addition, he thought about his son who'd become a big concern these past few years. He hadn't had a steady, bona fide job and he had refused to attend a trade school or university. *How does a father deal with a problem like that?* He felt stymied, but now, thanks to George, things had changed. He was hired to work in the fire department. Several weeks ago he had finished his training and now was the new rookie at Station No. 5.

He also thought about the firefighter who had been charged with molestation, was fired and then cleared. It was lucky for Hadley that he had reinstated him as quickly as he did or he would've had to answer to the union for it. *Oh well, it's all water under the bridge. New things on the agenda now,* he thought.

He had some great news to share with George and decided he would make that the focus of his visit. The other—the big issue he needed to discuss eating his gut— had to be broached with diplomacy so best it be treated as an afterthought.

When Chief Hadley received a call from Don's secretary booking an appointment for his visit, he knew something was up. He was filled with apprehension because whenever Don wanted to talk to him, he merely picked up the phone. Something *was* up, he could feel it in his bones.

When Don arrived he received a hearty handshake; he was asked to take a seat in the den and was offered a cup of coffee. Don could never turn down a cup of coffee and would drink it at every opportunity. He took a seat in the new, leather-bound easy chair directly across from Chief Hadley. "So, Don, to what do I owe the pleasure of your visit today?" asked Hadley.

He wanted to get right to the nitty-gritty and hoped the phoney smile on his face didn't betray him and expose his apprehension.

"Oh, there are a couple of things I need to discuss with you, George," said Don, shifting a bit in his chair to adjust the girth that had crept around his middle over the years.

"First of all, I want to compliment you on the success you are having with the calendar sales. This city has to be very proud of our firefighters. The money is rolling in. The burn unit at the hospital will be shocked when we give them the cheque. I would like you to present it to them next Friday at their annual benefit, appreciation dinner. I hope you and the missus will be able to attend."

"Of course, we haven't missed one yet. Do you have the latest total?"

"Brace yourself, George. Last count, and mind you it's still climbing, was fifty-two thousand dollars."

George stood up so quickly, he almost spilled his coffee. "You've got to be kidding! Fifty-two thousand dollars, that's phenomenal!" He sat down again beaming at his visitor. He was very proud indeed.

"Yes, for some reason sales have quadrupled over the last year. Every outlet is asking for more. Perhaps it's because there's been publicity of late with the ladder accident and the baby delivery."

"I didn't realize the baby thing got publicity."

"It sure did! All the ladies at City Hall and the court-house are pointing out the firefighter on the calendar who delivered the baby."

"That would be Garth Winters. Despite his rough start, he has turned out to be an excellent employee, and in many different ways. I have great staff at Station 5."

"He sure is popular with the ladies, I'll give him that. And, speaking of the staff at Station 5, I really appreciate your fast-tracking my son into a job. How's he making out?"

"He's doing just fine. He's on the quiet side but then he's just getting to know the crew . . . and the work."

The two men chatted on several different subjects, including sports and the weather. George knew Don was just passing time before the shoe would drop. Finally, Don stood up and started for the door.

"Thanks for chat and the coffee. I must be off. I have business to attend to back at City Hall. I hope you'll join our table at the benefit next week."

"We'll be happy to, Don." He walked with him to the door and then Don stopped and turned round.

"I almost forgot. I have something else to discuss with you. And I have to be honest, it is very serious indeed."

"What is it?"

"I think you better sit down."

Here it comes! The shoe is hitting the floor!

George followed his instruction and sat back down. Don stood before him, reached into his pocket and handed him a pin about two inches round with an attached clasping pin on the back. When he turned it over, George gasped. There, before him, printed on the bright yellow face were the words: "I got laid in the fire hall."

"W-where on earth did you get this damn thing?"

"It was on my desk when I arrived at work yesterday. I have no idea who put it there but someone was definitely trying to tell me something. If the media get their hands on this, it'll put the reputation of firefighters in serious jeopardy, not to mention our city. I have to be honest with you, George, this thing has been plaguing me and I hated having to tell you."

"No, no, no! You had to tell me and now I have to get to the bottom of this! The last thing we want is to have the public think we are being paid with public funds, and . . . and doing this!" He pointed at the pin and held it up. "And when I get to the bottom of this, heads are going to roll. In the meantime, Don, I think it's best you pretend you didn't see this. Just leave it with me."

Don shook his hand and left. George went back to his desk and put his head in his hands as he thought about how he was going tackle this new conundrum. He was still trying to deal with the aerial accident and now—this!

What to do? What to do?

He quickly made up his mind for his first course of action. By Monday morning he was anxious to meet with all his district chiefs. They would surely have an answer or solution to this dilemma. He knew Chief Watson from Station 5 would be one who would have quite a lot to say about it.

They were all waiting for George when he walked into the boardroom—a room where many problems were solved. It was also a room where new ideas were generated. Most recently they spoke at length about the aerial catastrophe with wise and thoughtful solutions for future training. But this new topic—this scandalous, unthinkable subject—was never raised in the past.

He helped himself to a cup of coffee from the sideboard and took his place at the head of the table.

"Good morning, gentlemen." Despite an almost sleepless night, he made every attempt to remain upbeat.

"I have been presented with a huge problem. Last Friday I had a visit from Don Symington, and as you all must know by now, he is the city administrator—and therefore our boss. Recently, there was a little unwrapped present anonymously put on his desk, which has placed all of the firefighters in this city under suspicion."

He paused to catch his breath and Chief Watson piped up.

"Suspicion? Of what?" His voice laid heavy on the 'what'.

"Yeah!" echoed the men around table. "Of what?"

"Prostitution!" declared George with a pound of his fist on the table. The men jumped in their chairs. They had never seen Chief Hadley so irate!

"Can you imagine? We are the life savers and firefighters for the people of this city and *we* are accused of prostitution. It will be one son of a bitch if the papers ever get hold of this one!"

A vein was visibly popping on his neck.

"What proof is there?" demanded District Chief Watson. "I'd like to see some proof."

George reached into his pocket for the pin which was passed around the table. One by one, the men naturally began to snicker.

"This is no laughing matter!" George exclaimed.

Comments came from around the table:

"How do we know it's not just a silly prank?"

"Yeah, how do we know? We beat Eggleston's Station No. 1 in curling last week and they were really pissed. How do we know they just didn't set us up?"

The district chief from Station No. 2 spoke loudly from the end of the table, doing his utmost to disguise a smile: "I'd like to know how this? This little pin can be proof of prostitution?"

George's voice took on a tone very close to a whisper: "What's the difference, you engage a lady for sex and you give her money. *Or* you entice her to come to the city's fire hall and reward her with this pin?"

He looked at the pin with repugnance and curled his bottom lip down and outward. Although his rhetoric was a mite farfetched, he did receive acquiescence from his district chiefs. He continued. "Now, the questions remaining gentlemen are: What are we going to do about it? Who is generating these disgusting pins? What stations are involved? With the strong code of brotherhood amongst the men, they will not squeal on one another, we know that for sure. We have to figure out a way to catch the culprit."

"I agree," said the chief from District 3. "We have to figure out a way ourselves."

"Yes," substantiated Chief Watson. "It's up to us," leaving thoughts to run rampant in his head.

"Alright then," said George. He stood up. "You have your mandate and I've been given mine. When we meet again in two weeks, I hope we have this thing solved."

District Chief Watson drove back to Station 5 in nothing less than a stupor. It was hard for him to concentrate on his driving and he nearly had an accident. Now, as he sat at his desk deep in thought, an idea struck him. Garth Winters was dating a girl from City Hall, was he not? Kyla, Kyla, whatsername? He needed to talk to Garth to see if he may have heard something about the pin, or perhaps this Kyla girl may have.

"First, I'd like to compliment you on delivering that baby. Some of us never get that opportunity. It's a feather in your cap for sure," stated Watson.

He studied the countenance of Garth Winters who had so quickly responded to his request to come to his office. His face showed a mixture of curiosity and attentiveness.

"Thanks," replied Garth. "Just doing my job."

"I need to ask a big favour of you."

He was thinking, *I hope I'm using the right approach.* "Along with the other District Chiefs, I have a huge problem to sort out, so I'm hoping you can help me."

"Be happy to, Chief. What can I do for you?"

District Chief Watson admired the young man sitting before him and once again could see great things in the future for him. It was his no nonsense, quiet dignity that impressed him the most. He knew Garth was a man to be trusted.

"It is vitally important we be discreet about this. I know you will keep this hush, hush." He shifted in his chair.

Garth levelled his gaze at his superior and nodded, making a curl fall over his forehead. "But of course."

"OK then, that's great. I'm going to get right to the point. The city administrator paid a visit to Chief Hadley last Friday and he gave him this pin."

He took the pin out of his pocket and handed it to Garth. Garth blinked and drew his head back.

"I thought I'd seen everything, but this really takes the prize," he said and stifled a chuckle.

Watson continued: "What I really need to do, Garth, is find out who's behind this. The reputation of firefighters is at stake."

He paused and waited for Garth's reply.

"How do we know it's our district? Could be any one of the others," Garth responded,

"Let's just say it's my hunch. There's a lot of tomfoolery going on in this district on a regular basis."

Garth had to agree. He recalled all the incidents he'd witnessed and heard about since coming to Station 5, but he had yet to hear about pins.

The chief continued: "I've been giving how to handle this situation a lot of thought. Then I thought about you. I have to say, Garth, I have a lot of respect for you and I know you can be trusted. What I would like to do is give you the mandate of finding out who is behind this caper and then put a stop to it. I know you'll come up with something."

"If I do find out, are you expecting me to tell you who it is?"

"No, no, I realize you have a brotherhood to protect. Remember, I was out fighting fires too before I became chief and still do from time to time. I haven't forgotten the importance of compatibility and camaraderie when one's life is on the line, both for the firefighters and the fire victims. No, no, I don't want to know who it is. What I would like you to do is let me know when you feel this mission, I'm entrusting to you with, has been accomplished."

The chief stood up indicating the meeting was over and extended his hand. Garth shook it with enough intensity to tell the chief, he had a deal. He picked the pin up off the desk and put it in his pocket.

Back in the coffee room, he filled a mug of coffee and joined the men at the table. He cupped his mug with both hands and took long draws while looking at the men around the table, all of whom he'd worked with, all he considered his brothers. He sat quietly evaluating each one wondering if any were connected with the pin. He knew them well except for the one new face—the son of City Administrator Don Symington. The rookie, Chad, seemed like a quiet, shy man who only spoke when spoken to. But he was still a rookie, who had joined the group in the past two weeks in replacement of Lance.

And of course, there was the one lady, Joan Radcliff, who always perched at the far end with her coffee and some-times a magazine. She was here for only a month replacing one of the guys who'd taken holidays. She was a seasoned firefighter; one of a handful of women the city employed as firefighters.

He looked at all the others again, trying to place some kind of characterization on each to be able to list them as a potential suspect, but to no avail.

Later, back at his apartment, he thought of Kyla. The pin came from City Hall, so perhaps she, or one of her co-workers, had some knowledge of it. He was seeing her later that evening and then he could ask her. He would explain how important it was to be discreet. Garth knew he could take her into his confidence. The plan for the evening was to go out for dinner and return to her apartment to watch a movie.

When they were leaving to go for dinner, and were about to pull out of the driveway, she declared, "Oh darn it, Garth, I have to go back in. I left my purse in the apartment."

He replied, "Take your time going but hurry back."

She laughed and called over her shoulder, "You are just too funny, Mr. Winters."

Over dinner at their favourite Italian restaurant, Garth started the conversation: "How many employees do you have at City Hall?"

"The last payroll I processed, there were thirty-two in total. That doesn't include the administrators or those on the council."

"How many men compared to women?"

Garth dove into his lasagna with gusto. Pasta always hit the spot when he was hungry.

"Let me see, there's one, two, three, four. Four, I guess that's it. Only four men, all the rest are women. Why, Garth? Are you thinking of changing employment?" She smiled and her brown eyes were sparkling.

Garth laughed. "Hell no, I like my job. Just curious, actually I do have a reason for asking. When we get back to your apartment, I'll explain it all."

"Now you've really piqued my curiosity," said Kyla, raising her eyebrows.

"Nice to know I can do that. One has to keep the little lady guessing." His grin made her heart flutter.

When they arrived at her apartment, Kyla opened a bottle of red wine and poured two glasses. She was anxious to hear what Garth had to say.

"What a lovely Christmas tree you have, Kyla, and so nicely decorated," said Garth.

Her sweet voice was mixed with laughter when she replied, "Oh, some nice firefighter stomped deep in the woods, through heavy snow and chopped it down, just for little ole me."

She handed him a glass of wine. Placing it on the coffee table, he sat next to her on the sofa and took her hand.

"I have to tell and ask you something, but first I need to establish what we talk about will be strictly confidential and will not leave this room. It is very important that you discuss this with no one. I know I can trust you, but I do need you to give me your word."

"But of course, Garth, you have my word." Her eyes had grown large with wonderment.

"I have been given an assignment by the district chief to investigate a very disturbing situation within the fire department."

"Really?" said Kyla.

"Yes, and it's important I get to the bottom of it as soon as possible. Something was placed on your administrator's desk that prompted him to visit our chief."

"What was it?" asked Kyla, now more curious than ever.

"This." Garth reached in his pocket and pulled out the pin and showed it to her.

I got laid in the fire hall.

"Oh, for Heaven's sake," Kyla's face turned red.

"On Symington's desk!" she laughed. "That's just too funny. I bet he had a hissy fit. He's such an old fuddle-duddy!"

She looked at the pin again and giggled.

"It's really nothing to laugh about, love. Think of the ramifications if the press gets wind of this. That's why we *must* keep it a secret—can't tell a living soul."

Garth put emphasis on, *must.*

"Have you seen this before, Kyla? Has there been any mention of pins amongst any of the girls in your office?"

"I've never laid eyes on that before or even heard of it. Gee whiz, Garth, it could have come from anywhere. There are countless people in and out of City Hall on a daily basis, from many different businesses and trades. People who have travelled around the world, people who have patronized sex stores and joke shops. It didn't have to originate from a firefighter."

"You're right, sweetheart, and that's what I have to prove. On the other hand if it has come from a firefighter, it could be deemed as payment and therefore a form of prostitution. Certainly not what the public wants to perceive as what goes on in their fire halls."

"How do you plan to find out?" She looked at him in earnest. Garth found the expression on her face so appealing.

"Well, that's where I need your help. I want you to keep your eyes and ears open, especially in the lunch room with all the other ladies. See if you can hear them talking about a pin or even about firefighters."

"Oh, wait just a moment." She covered her face with her hands. "Come to think of it, Garth . . . oh, why didn't I think of this earlier. About a week ago one of the girls by the name of Shirley asked me if I was still going out with a firefighter and then said something about a pin and just at that moment the buzzer rang. I didn't get a chance to ask her what she meant and then I forgot about the whole thing until just now. I can ask her tomorrow. I usually see Shirley at break."

"Great!" Garth squeezed her hand.

"I can also bring up the fire hall and firefighters in a pre-conceived conversation and perhaps will see how many girls have dated firefighters. I'll not breathe a word about the pin of course."

"I appreciate that. I know you'll be careful."

They sipped on their wine and before tuning into a movie on the television, Garth excused himself to go to the wash-room. She told him to take his time going but to hurry back and laughed. He turned and said, "Hey, you can't say that! It's my line!"

"Oh really, so you own the whole dictionary do you now, Mr. Winters?" The sound of her laughter warmed his heart. Sparring verbally with Kyla was fun.

In the bathroom, on the vanity he spied a ring holder spiking through a multitude of rings of all descriptions, just what he needed. He selected a small pearl ring from the bottom and slipped it into the change pocket of his wallet. He hoped she wouldn't miss it. He only needed it for a day, just long enough to find out what size she wore. He had another mission far more important than the one given to him by the chief and that was to buy an engagement ring for Kyla. And very soon he would plan an evening in which he'd ask her to marry him. He appreciated her old-fashioned values and wanted to do things just right.

But first he had to act like Detective Sherlock Holmes and find the cockroach who initiated that nasty little pin.

CHAPTER

17

THE NEXT DAY KYLA LEFT FOR THE OFFICE WITH A mission of her own. She so badly wanted to help Garth solve this troubling mystery and was going to do her best toward that end. As a matter of fact, she was beginning to feel very much like a sleuth.

The first part of the morning was dragging slower than a tortoise in the sand but she kept busy typing business letters for Mr. Symington and logging in the hours for the next payroll. At long last, the buzzer blew and it was time for coffee.

When she entered the coffee room, the table was buzzing with chatter. She glanced at all the girls sitting around the table. Ironically, they were all about the same age—some brunettes, some blonds real or otherwise, and one freckled-faced, chubby redhead.

Most of these ladies were single girls, a few married and some divorced. But Kyla did not see Shirley and felt a pang of disappointment. But then at last she came sauntering in, swinging her hips in a too-tight skirt and skin-tight, red sweater displaying cleavage that verged on indecency. Kyla was surprised the personnel officer hadn't chastised her for her attire. Perhaps the new human rights law had precluded it.

In response to someone's comment about her being late for coffee, she retorted, "I had to make an important phone call; don't do it on company time like some ladies I know." She winked broadly at her inquisitor to indicate jest.

Kyla viewed her distastefully but her mission took precedence. She invited her to come and sit in the empty chair next to her. Shirley smiled and walked over.

"How ya doing, Kyla? Is the old man keeping you busy these days?"

"Oh yes, as always. How about you in the licensing end of things? I hear there's a lot of new construction of late?"

"Yup, I'm really busy. I like it that way, makes the week go by quickly. And I get to see some big dude contractors with fat wallets." She smiled impishly.

"I bet you look forward to your weekends like I do."

"Sure do, there's always something happening. I love the weekends."

"Are you dating any one special?"

"Heck no, just playing the field."

"I've been meaning to ask you something, perhaps it's better if I call you at home tonight or we can drop by the lounge after work."

"I'd like that. See you at the front door after work and then we can decide where to go from there."

At 4:30 PM the buzzer rang and within minutes the City Hall's civil servants could be seen exiting the building, one after the other. Kyla found Shirley waiting at the front door as planned.

"Oh, there you are, Shirley. Well, where should we go?"

"I don't know about you but I'd love a beer around about now. Let's go to Jake's Bar."

"OK by me," said Kyla.

Jake's Bar, centred in the downtown area, was a hangout for singles and married folk alike. Many of the local employees frequented the preppy bar on a regular basis, firefighters among them.

They walked in and took a seat at the back. Shirley ordered a beer and Kyla a tonic.

"What! You're not having a real drink?" asked Shirley.

"Maybe I will later. Right now, I'm just thirsty for a tonic. I finished a big stack of letters this afternoon."

"What is it you wanted to talk to me about?" asked Shirley, hoisting up her chest and adjusting her sweater while eyeing a man across the room.

"About three weeks ago—when you found out I was going out with a firefighter—you mentioned something about a pin; about whether I'd got my pin yet and I didn't know what you meant. Before I could ask you the buzzer rang. It's been bugging me ever since."

Shirley threw her head back and laughed. "You mean you're going out with a firefighter and you haven't heard about the pin? Tell me you're kidding. You've gotta be kidding."

Kyla laughed with her. She wanted to appear congenial despite feeling anything but. "It's the truth . . . I haven't got a clue but I'd love to find out. Tell me, do you have a pin?"

"You bet your little booties I do, and I plan to get another."

"What exactly is the pin?"

"The only way I can explain it is to show you mine. And I'm hoping to get another."

She reached into her purse and pulled out the yellow pin, turned it over and proudly placed it on the table before Kyla like she was displaying an Olympic medal.

Kyla's feigned surprise was the standard of an Academy Award. She brought both hands to her cheeks and gasped, "Oh, for God's sake! What did you have to do to get this?"

Shirley looked at her in disbelief and said quite loudly, laying on the second syllable: "Ky-la!"

"Oh, I didn't mean it that way. What I meant is where did you get this?" said Kyla tripping over her words and feeling a flush creep up over her face.

"I'm told the source has to be a secret but I can tell you how to get one. All you have to do is hang around this place on the weekend. There's a firefighter who comes in on a regular basis looking for recruits. I think I'm the only one so far . . . no, that's not true, I think there's was one more."

"Can you at least tell me something about this guy? Is he tall? Short? Handsome? Ugly? Or what?"

"He's medium height, dark hair, ordinary-looking guy. Wears glasses and is hornier than a four-peckered owl."

Shirley's laughter rang out through the bar. She was laughing more at the shock on Kyla's face than what she'd just said.

"Can you at least tell me what station he comes from? I won't tell a soul. You have my word of honour."

Kyla held up her hand in a Girl Guide's salute, feeling very much like a hypocrite.

Shirley was quietly and carefully studying Kyla's face. She knew she held a very important job in City Hall being the private secretary to the Big Kahuna, Symington.

"I won't tell you but I'll give you a clue and you can take it from there."

"Shoot," said Kyla, excited now that she was making headway.

At this juncture, Shirley grinned ever so mischievously and held up her right hand spreading her fingers.

Kyla said she'd try to figure that out. "Hey, Shirley, thanks for the clue." She looked at her watch. "I must go. It's heading onto dinner time. Thanks again."

"Think nothing of it."

Both girls stood up. Shirley drained the last drops of her third beer and then Kyla led the way to the door. As she was exiting she looked over her shoulder and saw Shirley had lingered behind and was talking to the man at the back of the room.

When Kyla entered her apartment, she picked up the phone and called Garth to tell him the news. "Darling, the pin originated from Station Five." If Kyla felt like a sleuth, Garth felt like Sherlock Holmes.

The next day at the station, Garth took his place with the men at the coffee table. He hung around when the shift changed and appraised the men that came on. There were four platoons so it was next to impossible to evaluate them all. He had to put his thinking cap on.

If I were going to have sex in the fire hall, where could I do it? Couldn't be in the dorm. No privacy there. Couldn't be in the television room. Too many people always around. But, where? Where? Oh, I know the Watch Box, of course. The Watch Box! There's a side door in which they could be snuck in. It is far away from everything and very private and then there's the convenience of the bed. If it wasn't against the law and holding a ton of ramifications, I would put a camera in there.

Garth felt confused and for the next couple of days, he pondered what to do. He didn't want to give up; he wasn't going to give up, it was just not his style. On the third day his luck changed.

He was restless one night and was looking out the window when he saw the lady firefighter, Joan Radcliff, walking around the yard outside. Obviously she was restless too and needed some fresh air. He watched her walk around the parking lot. She walked past the window of the Watch Box and then began to hurry into the station, as if something had alarmed her. Garth quickly pulled on his trousers and went out into the hallway to intercept her.

"What is it, Joan?" he asked. She was flushed and also flustered.

"There's a naked lady in the Watch Box and she's making out with the firefighter that's on duty. Good grief. What's the world coming to?"

Garth hurried back to his room to put on his shirt when a call came in.

"Fire at 1630 St. George Street!

Repeat: Fire at 1630 St. George Street!"

There's nothing like a call to wake up the fire hall. Men scurried to the pumps, Garth included. He stopped quickly at the Watch Box just in time to see a blond lady hopping on one leg as she tried to pull a pair of jeans over her plush, bare backside. He yelled at her, "Get the hell out of here and don't ever show your ugly ass around here again," then he jumped into the truck just as the doors were slamming shut. As they roared down the street with the sirens blaring, Shirley slunk out the side door of the fire station, shaking like a puppy dog out of water.

When Garth came to work the next morning, he went directly to the shift roster to check to see who was working in the Watch Box. He was fully surprised.

Now he had to finish his mission. He went into the coffee room and whispered in the ear of the villain: "I need to talk to you. Come out to the parking lot." He followed Garth out of the room.

"I'm going to tell you this and I'm only going to tell you once. If you bring another woman into the fire hall, I'll personally beat the shit out of you, you goddamn idiot. What the hell's the matter with you? Bribing women with pins and discrediting the fire department. And you better round up and destroy all of those fucking pins, because if I see any around, you're as good as dead. Do you understand me, you cockroach?"

Chad Symington—son of City Administrator Don Symington—cowered under the height and strength of Garth Winters. He mumbled, "Yes, yes, yes, Sir."

Garth surprised himself with his strong words. It wasn't often he'd ever had to resort to blunt profanity but that was the only language this bonehead would understand.

The last time he had an altercation with anyone was in training when Hawks cut off his oxygen. Then Garth laid him flat. Better than a year had passed since then, yet when it seemed like only yesterday. He was surprised to learn recently that Hawks was still employed by the fire department.

The next morning when Chief Watson came into work, he saw a note on his desk. He turned it over and read: Mission Accomplished! *Good for Garth,* he thought. He picked up the red phone, which rang directly in Chief Hadley's office.

"Good Morning! Watson here. I just want to let you know, Chief, the little problem with the pins has been solved."

"I hope you're right. That problem has been hanging over my head for days now."

"I know. I feel confident that it's over."

"Good news, man. Without divulging anything to my secretary, I'll get her to contact all the other district chiefs. All she has to say is that Chief Hadley is sending a message to report the problem's solved. Thanks, George."

When Chief Hadley hung up the phone, he breathed a sigh of relief and then reached for his phone and dialled Don Symington at City Hall.

"Hello, Don," he said. "I have some good news for you. You know that little business about the pins; well, the problem has been solved. There's no need to worry about it any further."

He could visualize him seated at his untidy desk smiling when he received the news.

"I'm glad to hear that. You know there was another reason why I wanted to get this thing cleaned up. From one father to another, I was having trouble with my son Chad, finding his way. He went from one job to another—just didn't seem to fit in anywhere. I encouraged him to join the fire department. Then when this pin thing came about, I thought I'd really thrown him to the wolves. I was beginning to wonder if my son was mixing with the wrong type of guys. I'm relieved to know all is well on the Old Frontier."

Chief Hadley felt his dander rising and struggled to keep control.

"I'll have you know, my firefighters are not the wrong type of guys! They put their life on the line every day helping others! They are brave men. Their training and hard work builds character, always measuring a cut above!"

His voice became a little louder with each word.

"Oh, but of course, I didn't mean it quite like that, old chum. I'm just happy this is all cleaned up. Thanks for letting me know."

Chief Hadley let the phone slide back into its cradle without saying goodbye.

Neither man knew the truth.

CHAPTER

18

FOR MANY YEARS, PAPILLON, LIKE MOST OTHER
cities, had been experiencing a housing shortage. Two years
earlier when government agencies had offered a subsidy,
it didn't take City Council long to jump to the offer. Over
two hundred, low-rental, row-housing units were built at
the edge of town in close proximity to schools and shopping. They were attractive living accommodation for single
parents with young families, and for young couples starting
their life together.

It was early afternoon when the call came in. There was
a fire in one of the units; the potential for a major disaster
was looming. Among the group of firefighters responding,
Garth was partnered on the Rescue Truck. Like always, they
departed the fire station in a flash.

When they arrived at the address, the ground floor was
fully engulfed in flames, which were coming out the front

door and windows. A dishevelled, foreign woman, who couldn't be any older than twenty, came running through the growing throng of onlookers to meet them. She was wringing her hands and shouting in broken English, "My kids, my kids! My kids are upstairs."

The two firefighters on the pump strung in a line to extinguish the flames while Garth and his partner took on the duty of rescue. He quickly established where the staircase was by checking with another tenant who confirmed all the units were the same and the stairs was directly ten feet across from the front door. Fully equipped to deal with the emergency, Garth and his partner fought their way through the flames and up the staircase calling out, "Fire department! Anybody here?" They listened for a response but heard none. The space was pitch black with smoke and morbidly silent. All Garth could think of was, *There's kids up here; we have to find them!* His heart was pumping.

"You start on that left side and I'll do the right," said Garth.

Both men made a thorough search of the upstairs rooms but they could not find anyone.

"Let's look under the beds once more," said Garth, desperate to locate the children.

Lying flat on his stomach Garth was able to reach way back under one of the king-size beds. He felt something— it was a cardboard box. He pulled it out and reached in and felt something soft and furry. He took the box to the window and could see six small kittens in the box, obviously deceased and overcome by smoke.

Was the lady actually saying, my cats and not my kids?

With her accent, one could not be sure. All flames on the main floor had been doused by the crew when Garth and his partner descended and walked back out.

Garth asked the woman if she meant cats and she nodded. Immediately, he could feel the tension and anxiety he had been experiencing for the past fifteen minutes ebb slowly away.

"I'm sorry to have to tell you but the kittens did not survive. We'll take the carcases away for you."

"Tank you," she murmured and walked away with her hands over her face.

"We need to put them in a garbage bag and tie it up and dispose of it," said Garth. "There are children outside; it wouldn't be good for them to see these dead kittens."

Having extinguished the fire, the rest of the crew were busy placing fans around by all the windows to help clear the smoke-filled air from the apartment. It was ascertained the fire was caused by a frying pan of oil igniting after being left on high heat. Fortunately, only the interior of one unit had been damaged.

The firefighters from Station No. 5 saved Papillon much needed rental units.

***

Garth and Kyla had been dating now for several months and planned to have a special dinner at her apartment to celebrate their relationship. She pleased him by wanting to cook his favourite meal—Irish stew.

Garth chose their favourite wine and, despite not taking the time to test its aroma, he selected a bottle of perfume called 'Lasting Love'.

He was smartly dressed for the occasion, wearing black dress trousers, white shirt and tie, black Melton coat with a maroon scarf.

Kyla had to catch her breath at the sight of her man. She wore a midnight blue, off the shoulder low-cut dress, hiding the curve of her breasts. Her hair fell softly to her shoulders and her eyes were brilliant in appearance.

"Hello, sweetheart," he said, handing her the wine and gift.

"Oh, you have a present for me? How wonderful!"

She set the wine on the hall table and walked into the living room. Garth removed his coat, hung it in the closet, and then joined her on the sofa. He watched as she began to carefully open her present, her face beaming with joy at the sight of the small, ornate bottle of perfume.

"How did you know? I love this perfume. Thank you so much." Garth smiled as he watched her smell the fragrance and then she leaned over toward him and kissed him.

They toasted each other at the candle-lit table and enjoyed the meal amidst lively conversation. Garth told her all about the conclusion of the pin saga. She wondered if the woman in the Watch Box was Shirley. She would never find out, however, as she'd heard Shirley had left City Hall and was now working for a contractor.

After dinner, the lights were dimmed in the living room and they danced slowly to the sound of soft music. It was a perfect evening.

He could feel her heart beating against his and wondered if she felt the same way about him. He stopped, and with both hands he turned her face up to his, and said, "I love you, Kyla, very much."

"I love you too, Garth." Kyla saw the love in his eyes and her heart skipped a beat. She took his hand and led him down the hallway to her bedroom.

The music from the living room could be heard faintly as they took off their clothes. Garth ran his fingers gently across her hips. He gazed upon the roundness of her breasts and upturned nipples and was anxious to cover them with his mouth.

Kyla gazed at his muscular physique and caught her breath as she felt his manhood press against her. She wanted to be possessed by him, to belong to him, to seal their love. A slow smile formed at the corner of his lips as he tilted up her chin to give her his arduous kiss. Breathlessly they fell back onto the bed and made passionate love before falling asleep entwined in each others arms.

CHAPTER

19

SPRING HAD ARRIVED AND THE FIREFIGHTERS AT Station No. 5 had survived one catastrophic event after another. They had saved lives and property and had lost a few but had managed to keep their spirits ready for whatever may come their way again.

It was a typical spring evening; the moon shone brightly and while the traces of winter air still lingered, a warmer climate was well on its way. Garth was on evening shift and upon retiring glanced out the window and was amazed how bright the parking lot appeared under the moonlight. He had barely crawled into bed when a call came in:

"Medical Aid needed at 50th Avenue and Bruce.

Repeat: Medical Aid needed at 50th Avenue and Bruce."

Oscar and Sally Robertson and their three children were visiting their cottage by the lake, preparing it for weekend getaways for the upcoming summer months. Their much-loved cottage was their home away from home and they always enjoyed spending time at this quiet, lovely place on the shore of Lake Reindeer.

They took inventory of all staple items, checked the plumbing and did a special cleaning of all the rooms: kitchen, bath, living room and the two bedrooms.

Sally's father, Bert Walters, had said that he would join the family at their cottage on Sunday morning, yet so far, he had failed to show up. Sally was worried. *Where is he? What's taking him so long?* She wondered frantically. Her father had insisted on staying back to attend to some business, but said that he would join them thereafter.

He had been run over on a crosswalk by a drunk driver two years earlier and was now in a wheelchair, but a good driver nonetheless. His van was specially designed so he could drive it. Being able to do so had given him a renewed sense of independence which the accident had taken from him. He often took little road trips to visit family and friends with his wheelchair tucked in the back. He loved the freedom to travel.

He was expected to arrive at the cottage Sunday morning; no later than one o'clock—two o'clock at the latest. It was five o'clock Sunday afternoon. If he'd left in the morning as planned, he should've arrived three hours ago. Sally and Oscar were beginning to panic. They waited until 7:30 PM and then called the next door neighbour back in Papillon to check on him.

Garth responded to the call. When he and his fellow fire-fighters reached the destination and pulled up in the drive-way, they saw a man in front of the garage. The man, notably shaken, greeted them saying, "He's in there. His daughter asked me to check on him. I live next door."

The first thing they saw when they entered the garage, was an elderly man with a rope around his neck at the far end of the garage hanging from the rafters, obviously dead. His mouth was open and his face was a shade between crimson and blue. Beneath him was a wheelchair tipped over sideways. Garth righted the wheelchair and assisted in cutting the rope. They gently lay the man down on the floor of the garage, then called the police knowing they in turn would contact the coroner.

The neighbour handed Garth three pages of foolscap.

"I found this on the workbench. It's his suicide letter."

Garth thought, *I wish people wouldn't touch things at the scene.*

"Thank you," he said taking the pages. He started to read and wished he hadn't. He stopped reading for a moment but he wanted to know why someone would do this, so continued. He could see a lot of time was taken in writing the letter. The handwriting was perfect, equal to that of a calligrapher.

While Garth admired the superb penmanship, it was the content that impressed him most; it would stay with him a lifetime. He passed it to the other first responders.

My dearest Sally,

I have loved you from the first time I laid eyes on you in the hospital. Such a beautiful little girl you were, and as I watched you grow up, I thought my heart would burst with pride. You and I each had a role to play, you as a daughter and I as a father. You did a much better job than I.

Thank you so much sweet girl for being so good to me after my accident. I hated being a burden to you. You do not deserve to have a burden. Please forgive me for doing this. You see, last Friday when I was at the doctor, he gave me some very bad news. He said a fast growing cancer has developed in my right leg where it was amputated. He gave me only three months to live. I just couldn't put this burden on you. I've had some terrible pain for some time now and I know it will only get worse. I will be so miserable, which would be hard on you and your family. Please forgive me, Sally. I love you beyond words. Again, please forgive me. It is the best thing for me and for your family for me to do this now. If only assisted suicide were possible, we all could have been party to this, but that's not the way it is . . . please forgive me.

Dad.

Dear Oscar,

When you first met Sally and started taking her out, I have to tell you I did not like you. I didn't think you were good enough for my girl. And when you got married, I found it so hard to accept you as a son-in-law. Forgive me for telling you this, but I felt that way for a long time. It wasn't until you and Sally had your first child that I saw what a good father you are, and also what a good husband you had become, that I started to like you. I now know you make Sally happy and that is all I could ask for. I also know you will give her the support she needs when she gets the news of my death. I'm truly sorry to have to do this Oscar, but I really have no choice.

Bert.

Dear Linda,

I want you to know I think you are beautiful, bright teenage girl with a lifetime of success ahead of you. Please forgive Gramps for making you sad now. Your mother will explain to you why it has to be this way.

In the future, I want you to always be good to your parents, give them respect even when you feel angry at them. As you grow older you will understand why they give you some difficult rules to follow. Do your very best in school. How you study and apply yourself makes all the difference in the world in what marks you receive. And how well-educated you are makes the difference of living poor or in comfort. Most of all remember that contentment is the best measure of success. All the best darling girl. I love you.

Gramps.

Dear Darren,

I have enjoyed going to your ball games. You are a pretty, darn good ball player. Keep up with your sports because it is a real character builder. Please forgive Gramps for leaving. I will miss your ball games. I admired the way you cut the lawn for your parents. You are a good lad. Do your best in school. An education is most important. Try to choose a career where you know you will easily get employment.

Always be good to your Mom and Dad and brother and sister. Take care of them when you can and don't let anyone hurt them. I am sorry if my departure makes you sad, but really it is for the best. Your Mom will explain it to you. Just know I love you.

Gramps

Dear Alex,

I loved looking at your butterfly collection. I think you should keep doing it because you enjoy it so much. I am sorry that I have to leave. Your Mom will explain it to you. I hope that life is good to you and that you will grow up to be a big, strong man someday. Love your family always—they are your gold nuggets of life. Always respect and listen to your parents and always do your best in school.

Love from Gramps.

The police arrived and the firefighters left the scene, each with tears in their eyes.

While the firefighters enjoyed the tomfoolery that went on at the station, the day had now taken on a more sombre tone.

Garth and his crew talked about yesterday's sadness and others at the table began relating suicide events they'd attended or heard about:

"Last week, a captain in another platoon had to be called out to a report of a teenager that was up a tree bleeding. When they arrived there was blood down the trunk and on the ground. He was trying to castrate himself with a tin can. They managed to get him down the tree and into an ambulance. A family member reported he had made his young girlfriend pregnant."

"On a Saturday morning in December, a call came for medical aid. The mother reported that her son, who was nineteen years old, was depressed. He had a pistol and was planning to shoot himself. He was downstairs and probably still had the gun. There was a policeman on site but he wouldn't go down into the family room until his back-up arrived.

"But we firefighters went down and peeked through the door of the family room. Her son was sitting in a chair with blood running down his head from many wounds. The gun wasn't in sight.

"I approached, knelt down in front of him and started a conversation. He only stared straight ahead like he was in a daze. I asked where the gun was. He glanced at the table lamp and I guessed it was under the base. Sure enough, there it was—a starter pistol. He had fired seven wads into his forehead. That only broke the skin. His mother had traced the trail of blood out to the garage where there was a suicide note. He was a college student and it was shortly before Christmas and he was worried about exams; worry had put him in this frame of mind."

"It really surprises me how someone could be so despondent that they would consider taking their life, like the college boy, for example."

"Yeah, like the kid up the tree. Can you imagine that? A tin can? Yikes! I think I'd just stick a hose on the exhaust and go out the easy way. Frankly, I think he just wanted attention and had to make himself bleed to get it."

"Now, the wheelchair case is quite a different story," said another. "I think if I knew I was dying and there was no hope for me, I'd want to go."

"There have been a lot of cases but the law against assisted suicide stands strong."

"I think it should be lifted. Surely a person should have the right to say when he or she dies."

"I have a different school of thought as I keep thinking there might be a miraculous cure for some of those ailments. Research is going on all the time and coming up with cures."

"I think the general populace is afraid the bar will be lifted and in time, decisions to kill off the crippled, weak, and elderly will occur."

"That's a load of bunk. I think . . ."

The conversation came to an abrupt halt when a call came in:

"Fire in the underground parking lot at 1710 St. Andrew Street."

The firefighters ran to the apparatus room, donned their bunker gear and were off leaving their unfinished, controversial conversation behind.

On approach, black smoke was visibly coming out of the underground parking lot. They quickly strung a line.

As they entered they could see a sleek, black Lincoln Continental exuding heavy, dark smoke from beneath its hood. They needed to open the car doors to pop the hood but the doors were locked. Fortunately, firefighter Dave Hanson was with them and he was working part-time for a locksmith. It didn't take him long with a couple of tools to unlock the door and pop the hood.

They had to jump back when the vehicle burst into flames from the insurgence of oxygen. Fortunately, Dave, who was the closest, made the backward leap before the flames hit him. Despite water being sprayed, they knew it wouldn't take long for the gas tank to explode so they had to be extra cautious. The owner of the vehicle came running. His booming voice echoed throughout the underground lot.

"That's my car! That's my car! How the hell did you guys get into my vehicle? I paid extra money to ensure it was fool-proof. How the hell did you get into it? Damn it anyway!"

He was much more alarmed about the entry than the loss of his beautiful car.

The men talked about it all the way back to the station and all they could say was, "Go figure!"

CHAPTER

20

EVERY WINTER, ROBERT RUSHFORD, A FIREFIGHTER from Station No. 5, was one of those lucky men who could take his family, his camper and his boat to Camp Mikasue in California. Although he was only gone for a short spell it still gave him a reprieve from the blustering cold of Saskatchewan.

With his wife and their two young children, they parked in a lovely campground where the lake was so clear one could see the bottom many feet out from the shore. They swam, relaxed in the warmth of the sun, and always came back rested and rejuvenated.

It was early morning, the day they were returning to Canada. Robert drove down to the dock to hitch up his boat for the drive home. As he was walking along the dock to where his boat had been moored, he glanced down into the water and saw a child's body beneath the surface.

Instantaneously, he took off his shoes, jumped into the water and dove under. He brought the body up to the surface and immediately began resuscitation. He hollered to the crowd that was gathering, "Call 911."

Water began spewing from the child's mouth like a small fountain as he persistently worked on him. Soon sirens could be heard in the distance but the sound of a feeble cry from the child was music to Robert's ears. When his limp body began to move a little, Robert exclaimed, "That's my boy!"

The first responders on the scene took him away by ambulance and Robert returned down the shore to his car and boat. With boat in tow, the family of four left in their recreation vehicle. They were leaving their winter retreat in California and returning home to Canada.

***

Sarah Coleman, a widow of fourteen months was still grieving from the loss of her husband John, who'd died in a plane crash. Not a day passed that she didn't count her blessings for Jimmy, the wonder child they had waited so long to have.

"Jimmy, Jimmy, where are you? Jimmy, come here. It's time for breakfast. I have your porridge ready. Come and get it!"

Her voice was musical.

He wasn't responding. It wasn't like him. He usually came running where food was concerned. They had come camping because this was something John had promised the boy. He was so excited about coming on this holiday. He referred to it as "living with the trees".

She pulled up the flap on the tent and stepped inside— his sleeping bag was empty.

"Jimmy, Jimmy! Are you hiding somewhere? Please don't tease Mommy."

There was no response. Sarah began to panic. She began running around the campsite calling his name. People were eating their breakfast and the aroma of coffee and toast had filled the air but she did not notice. Her heart was in her throat. All she could think of was that someone had stolen her little boy. He loved the water; perhaps he went to the lake, but he knew he was not allowed to go there without her. Didn't she drill that into him when they arrived?

"Did you see a little boy this high, blond hair?" she asked everyone she saw, holding back the tears as she spoke. One ugly thought occupied her mind, *What if I never find him? I cannot live without him! He is all I have—all I have left of John. Please God.*

When she reached the shore she was crying uncontrollably. She saw a scrum of people on the wharf and a police car with strobe lights blazing.

"My little boy is missing, please help me! He's four years old, blond. He's a beautiful little boy!"

The policeman was happy to tell her: "Ma'am, a little boy has just been rescued out of the water. Yeah, he was blond and I thought about five years old and about this tall," he gestured with his hand. "The ambulance would have taken him to the local hospital. Step into my car, I'll take you there."

Trembling, Sarah climbed into his car and with a shaky voice asked, "W-w-was he alive? Was he OK?"

"The boy seemed fine to me," said the policeman. "The hospital will check him out. He was asking for you."

"Oh, poor Jimmy! Do you know who rescued him?"

"The man took off with his camper and boat before I could get his name. I think he was checking out of the campground. I asked around and no one knew him. He obviously wasn't going to stand around and take bows. My kind of hero!"

The conversation ended there. All that could be heard in the vehicle was sniffling from Sarah and radio calls for the policeman.

When they pulled up in front of the hospital, Sarah released a quivering sigh, got out of the car and ran to the front door. The policeman was right behind her. She was shown to the emergency room where she found Jimmy, who was sitting up in a bed. When he saw her, he began to cry.

"I'm sorry, Mommy," he said. "I know I wasn't supposed to be down at the lake. I don't know how I got there. I was dreaming that I was swimming."

She held him close to her chest and could feel his heart beating.

"You must have walked in your sleep so. All is OK. I'm so happy you're safe now."

The doctor kept Jimmy in the hospital overnight for observation, stating he wanted to keep a close eye on his lungs. His mother slept in the bedroom on a cot beside him, grateful beyond words she had not lost her son. One thought remained upper most in her mind: *I've got to find out who saved my boy so I can thank him.*

The next day Sarah and Jimmy returned to the camp-site. Sarah went to the camp office to inquire about who had registered.

"Can I help you?" asked the lady clerk.

"I'm trying to find out who saved my boy from drowning yesterday."

"Oh, I heard about that. Do you have any information or clues as to who it might be?"

"All I know is that he had a camper and a boat."

"Oh dear, just about everyone who comes in here has a camper and a boat."

"I also know he might have been checking out yesterday."

"At least fifty people checked out yesterday. This is a big campsite. There are two-hundred sites here. We are the largest this side of Palm Springs."

"Can we go over the list of those who left yesterday? You would have their contact information, would you not?"

"Yes, I have the departure list. I'll copy it for you."

Sarah thanked her for the list and then returned to the campsite with her son.

"We will be packing up to go home now, Jimmy. I have many phone calls to make to find out who saved you. We have to thank the man who saved your life."

He smiled at her and nodded. He wasn't quite back to normal since his ordeal, otherwise he would have protested.

Back at their home Sarah thought, *Perhaps the individual doesn't want to be recognized as a hero. Some people are like that. He may be shy about it and I may not get a straight answer. I'll ask them if they left Camp Mikasue yesterday and then ask if they know how to resuscitate a drowning victim. If they say no, they'll be struck off the list. If yes, then the next question I'll ask is: "Did you save a little boy at the dock in Camp Mikasue?"*

The phone calls turned out to be more complicated than she thought. She spent two hours on the phone and only managed to get through to about ten people. Many did not answer their phone. Many had answering machines but did not return the calls. Some were just plain rude. But Sarah wasn't daunted. She was going to find out who saved her son if it was the last thing she did on the face of the Earth. She kept on phoning and her left ear was beginning to ache.

On the second day, there was a small breakthrough. One of the men she spoke to said that there was a man in the campsite next to him who was a firefighter. All firefighters know how to give resuscitation. He also said he was from Canada and his licence plate read: Saskatchewan—The Land of Living Skies. He said he remembered that because it reminded him of Big Sky, Montana. He also remembered there was an X and a 3 in the plate number but couldn't remember the rest of it.

Now Sarah had something to go on. But there must be gazillion fire stations in Saskatchewan. How could she pin it down?

I know, she thought, *I'll inquire at our local fire station. They should be able to help me and give me some direction.*

"Hello, this is Sarah Coleman. I'm wondering if you can tell me how to find a particular firefighter in Saskatchewan,

Canada? Last week my son was saved from drowning at Camp Mikasue and I never had a chance to thank him."

"You'll need to talk to Chief Blair," said the receptionist. "He can help you better than I can. Boy, that's like trying to find a needle in a haystack."

Sarah didn't need to hear that glib remark.

"Chief Blair here, what can I do for you?"

Sarah related the story of the Canadian firefighter and her son. The chief listened intently.

"Well now, that will be a challenge. But I love a challenge," laughed the chief. "Let me think about it for a moment. First, I think it would be a good idea if we get the media involved. They can do wonders! Hmm, hmm, let me see. Oh yes, I think I can get a list of all the fire stations in that state, I mean province. There will be a lot of them. If only we could get the name of the city or town. That would make it easier. You said there was an X and 3 in the licence number. I know. Perhaps the motor vehicle branch in Saskatchewan could narrow it down further for us. I'll call them in the morning. Just leave your phone number with me."

"I'm ever so grateful," said Sarah as she wrote her phone number down on the pad on his desk.

"I like that man," said Jimmy.

"So do I," said Sarah.

Sarah waited all morning for the chief to call her back but the phone was silent. She gave Jimmy his lunch and paced around the room. When the phone did ring, she jumped and flew to right to it.

"Chief Blair here. Can I speak to Sarah, please?"

"This is Sarah." Her heart picked up a beat.

"I have some good news for you. The licence plate number has been narrowed down to a city by the name of Papillon in central Saskatchewan. There are nineteen fire stations in Papillon. You will have to call each station."

He spelled the name of the city for her and gave her the phone numbers. She read them back to him for accuracy.

"Good luck! Oh, by the way, Papillon means, butterfly in French. I looked it up."

She giggled and said, "That's good. Jimmy loves butterflies. I cannot thank you enough, Chief Blair."

"Don't mention it, always here to help."

***

Chief Watson was driving into work when an announcement on the radio caught his attention.

"Ladies and gentlemen, this is an important announcement. A Canadian firefighter bravely rescued and saved the life of a four-year-old California boy from drowning two days ago. After he made the rescue he disappeared and the boy's mother did not have a chance to thank him. If anyone knows his identity, please call this radio station."

Well what do you know. One of Canada's firefighters is a hero in the USA. I wonder what city he's from, and more importantly, what station. Wouldn't it be my stroke of luck if he were from No. 5?

Sarah began her telephone calls. This time her question to the chief at each station was, "Have any of your firefighters been on a holiday recently in the USA?"

She called two numbers with no luck, but the third time was, as they say, a charm.

"Yes," replied Chief Watson in response to her query. "As a matter of a fact, a firefighter from this station spent some time in California recently. He returned this morning. His name is Robert Rushford."

"He saved my son's life. I want to come to Canada to thank him. I never had a chance to before. He left so quickly."

"When do you plan to come? I can arrange to have the media on site when you do. They will love to have a human interest story. And I wouldn't mind a little publicity for the fire department."

The thought made him feel excited. He released a low chuckle.

"Let me see," said Sarah. "Today is Thursday. I can come next Monday. Does that give you enough time?"

"Yes, that will work but I would like your phone number in case I need to reach you. Please, let me know your time of arrival, I'll have someone meet you at the airport. I think it will be interesting if we surprise Robert."

"Thanks, I'll let you know my flight time."

***

When Garth Winters arrived at work on Monday morning, the parking lot was full.

Something is going down the pipe! he thought

There were media trucks everywhere including one from the USA. The lobby was packed with people and therefore he could barely enter the fire station. There was Head Honcho Hadley from upstairs, city officials, media people, chiefs from other stations, crew members from Station No. 5. It was surreal, like he was watching a movie. And then to his utmost astonishment, Kyla was there standing with her back against the wall looking as beautiful as ever. He inched his way over to her. The sight of her always made his heart race a little.

"This is a pleasant surprise. I wasn't expecting to see you here, or for that matter, all these other people. Do you know what's happening?"

"I think someone is getting an award of some kind but I'm not sure what. I wasn't expecting to be here either. My boss asked me to come at the last minute."

Garth reached for her hand and squeezed it. The hum of the crowd was interrupted by Chief Hadley clapping his hands for attention with District Chief Watson at his side. He spoke into the microphone that had been provided by the media.

"Ladies and gentlemen, could I have your attention please. I would like to thank you all for coming. Needless to say, we are very proud of our firefighter Robert Rushford, for his heroic act of saving a small boy when he was holiday-ing in California."

A buzz filled the room and one firefighter could be heard saying, "I heard about that on the news."

Chief Hadley continued: "He doesn't know we are gathering here today to honour him. I expect him to arrive in a few minutes. He's on the last day of his holidays. I phoned him and told him I needed to see him for an urgent matter. He will be very surprised, indeed. Most of all he will be surprised to meet the young boy and his mother. They are waiting in my office. I want you all to follow me into the apparatus room in the station; this is where the filming of the presentation will be held. The apparatus will make a great background."

Everyone clapped then followed Chief Hadley across the fire hall into the large apparatus room. He hoped a call wouldn't come in until the presentation was over. The filming producer walked over and conversed with Chief Hadley for a few minutes.

A call did come across the intercom. It was from the firefighter in the Watch Box.

"Chief Hadley, Robert Rushford is here to see you."

Hadley spoke into the microphone: "Ladies and gentlemen, Robert Rushford has arrived. I'll bring him here in a few minutes, as well as the mother and her son."

He left the room only to return shortly after with the hero firefighter in tow; standing behind the door out of sight, was the mother and her son. When Robert entered the room, everyone began to clap. Robert was baffled and all he could say was, "What's going on?"

Microphone in hand, the American broadcaster began speaking to the camera positioned in front of him. It would be on the news later that day, in several cities in the USA and Canada, and even in various cities around the world.

"Ladies and gentlemen, I am standing here in Fire Station No. 5 in Papillon, Saskatchewan, Canada. Two weeks ago at

Camp Mikasue in California, a brave, Canadian firefighter from this very station, saved a young American boy from drowning. He left the scene before the boy's mother had a chance to thank him. Since then she has been able trace him to this very fire station in Canada. Her name is Sarah Coleman, and along with her son Jimmy, they are here today to say thank you to firefighter Robert Rushford."

Everyone applauded. Wearing a broad smile, Chief Watson stood proudly beside Chief Hadley. The mother and child were brought into the room.

Robert stood dumbfounded. However, when he saw the grateful mother sobbing with gratitude, his eyes welled up, along with everybody else in the room. Sarah hugged Robert and he bent down to receive a hug from little Jimmy.

"There are no words to express my thanks," she said. "I could not have lived without my Jimmy."

She patted Jimmy's blond head. He looked up at her with clear-blue eyes and smiled sweetly.

"On behalf of all the firefighters in Mikasue, California, I would like to give you this award of merit. Thank you so very much for saving my son's life!"

She handed him a framed document.

Robert received it appearing somewhat embarrassed. The camera was focused on him now for his comments.

He looked into the camera and turned his attention to the mother and said, "I'm happy to have met you and Jimmy. Thank you for this award and for coming to Canada but it isn't necessary to thank me because saving lives is what a firefighter does."

The applause was instantaneous and lasted for several moments while the cameras were rolling.

When the crowd was slowly dispersing, Chief Hadley, District Chief Watson, City Administrator Don Symington, Robert, Sarah and Jimmy left for a pre-planned lunch at one of Papillon's best restaurants, The Golden Crock.

Garth walked Kyla to her car and gave her a peck on the cheek. "As soon as I have my days off, I want to take you out to a special dinner," said Garth through the car window.

"A special dinner? Now I'm going to be wondering what that's all about," she laughed.

"You're just going to have to wait and see, my sweet."

She gave him a sly look beneath her lashes and was beaming as she drove away.

The next day, Chief Watson sat at his desk, drinking his morning coffee with the Papillon Post spread out in front of him. Big letters in red at the top of the front page read:

HERO FIREFIGHTER SAVES AMERICAN BOY!

He also knew the story would be on the news. He quickly turned on the television and listened attentively. He couldn't remember when he'd felt so happy, or for that matter, so proud.

Ironically, Chief Hadley had a newspaper spread on his desk and was waiting to see the broadcast. When it came on the screen and he saw Robert Rushford receiving an award from the American mother and son, along with the crowd that had gathered in the apparatus room with the big red fire trucks as a backdrop, he felt honoured.

CHAPTER

21

ALL FIREFIGHTERS LOOKED FORWARD TO THEIR DAYS off when they could attend to their personal business, a special event with their families, or even a second job afforded to them because of a shift schedule giving generous days off.

In Garth Winters' case, it was his farmland in the country where he would spend most of his time. And in the next few days, he would make a lifelong commitment to the woman he loved and to the development of his country property.

At last the time had arrived and he was filled with excitement as he drove to Kyla's for their special date. She had picked a small French restaurant in the quiet end of town; it was a place he'd not been to previously, despite many good reports. But the evening held more than just fine dining; for Garth Winters, this was the first day of the rest of his life.

Kyla was radiant in a black, silk dress with a single string of pearls at her throat. Her eyes, as usual, were sparkling when he opened the door. He could smell her perfume when they embraced and felt his heart quicken as it always did when they were close.

They enjoyed a lovely dinner of Cordon Bleu accompanied by Sauvignon Blanc. There was only one other patron at the far end of the room giving them privacy.

Garth held Kyla's hands and commented: "My, this is a pretty ring, Kyla. It was the same one he had borrowed for a time—funny she hadn't missed it. He slipped the pearl ring from her finger and jokingly tried it on his little finger, which didn't get past the first knuckle. Laughing, he took her hand to put it back, but this time he replaced it with a large solitaire diamond with a miniature sapphire on each side. He kept one hand over hers and pocketed the pearl ring with the other. He amazed himself at how adept he was with sleight of hand. They kept on talking and laughing and all the while he had her hand with the diamond ring covered by his.

The waiter came and refilled their glasses. Holding her gaze he took both hands and whispered softly: "Kyla, I love you, and want to spend the rest of my life with you. Will you be my wife?"

Immediately her eyes filled with tears.

"I've been hoping you would ask me. I want to spend the rest of my life with you too, Garth. I can't imagine spending it with anyone else."

He was overjoyed. *Now my life begins*, he thought.

They both stood up and kissed across the table.

"I'm surprised you haven't noticed it."

"Noticed what, Garth?"

He glanced down at her hand. She followed his gaze and gasped, "Oh, my goodness! How did you? When did you? It's beautiful! I can't believe I didn't notice it sooner. I love it, Garth!"

She placed her palms together and closed her eyes, a vision that would remain with him for ever.

The next day they rode their horses, while chatting also about their future and planning their wedding for October. "Sweetheart," said Garth, "it won't be easy being married to a firefighter. While I will have a lot of days off in a row, there will be many days you will be alone at home with the children."

Kyla laughed and replied, "If we love each other, it won't matter. Just think of it as a mini honeymoon when you return." She laughed again, "By the way, I would like to have four children."

"You've got my vote," he said with blue eyes twinkling. They spurred their horses into a gallop and when they reined in their sweating steeds, Garth said, "By the way, you were supposed to give that little mare a name."

"That's easy. I'm going to call her Bullet. When I first rode her, you said she goes like a bullet and I've discovered she really does. Yes, I'm going to call her Bullet."

"Good name, Kyla. Most fitting."

Later at her apartment, he showed her an architect's design of a country home and asked for her input. Her only request was for a pantry in the kitchen.

"I love everything else about it. It's so exciting to have a new home built," she declared. "I can hardly wait. When are you starting it?"

"In a couple of weeks after the architect makes the adjustment for the pantry. I want it ready for us after our wedding."

"I'm so happy, Garth," she said.

"Me too, darling, and tomorrow, I would like to take you to Louie's Bar and Grill. They make the best chicken wings imaginable. While we munch on them, we can put some plans together for the wedding."

"That sounds wonderful, darling," she replied.

Louie's Bar and Grill, located in mid Papillon in close proximity to all the fire halls, soon had become a favourite hangout for the firefighters. It was there they celebrated promotions, honoured retirees and took advantage of the private rooms for many of their other special occasions.

Garth and Kyla ordered a bottle of Chardonnay and chicken wings and a salad. Garth excused himself to go to the men's room and Kyla took a notepad and pen out of her purse and began making a list, when a man's voice interrupted her thoughts.

"Haven't we met before? You look so familiar?"

Marvin Hawks had entered the bar and had quickly spotted Kyla sitting alone in the booth. He recognized her as the pretty girl who caught his eye at the calendar dinner-dance last fall and thought she was the loveliest thing he'd ever seen. Tonight was his lucky night; he didn't think he'd ever see her again. At last, he'd have a chance to make her acquaintance.

"No, we haven't," replied Kyla thinking, *Couldn't he be more original?*

"Well, I could have sworn we met. Oh, now I know, you attended the last firefighter's calendar dinner and dance."

Kyla laughed, "I was there but I didn't see you."

At that moment, Garth arrived at the booth. When Marvin saw him, he quickly escaped and made his way into the men's washroom. Garth was right behind. He pushed him up against the wall by his collar.

"Listen, you son of a bitch, you stay the hell away from my girl or I'll not only bust your jaw but this time I'll break both your arms!"

He released him, and before Marvin could say anything, Garth turned and walked out the door.

Cockroach!

Back at the booth, he had some explaining to do to Kyla for leaving so abruptly, but managed to smooth it over. They enjoyed a dinner while making plans for their wedding.

Garth's six days off began and finished in a flash. He returned to work on the evening shift, back to all the jargon of the guys at the table and to a dinner cooked by Bob, the best cook in the fire hall. He presented everyone with pork chops, mashed potatoes and broccoli, which were all done to perfection. He even made gravy from the drippings in the pan. While they ate heartily, conversation at the table centred on the new firefighter who was transferred in from Station No. 1.

"You're not going to be happy about this, Garth," they said.

Immediately, Garth thought it might be Hawks and was filled with dread.

"His name is Dennis Jones. He has the bunk right next to yours. I hear he sleeps in the raw—must have come from a nudist colony."

"Each to their own, guys. He can sleep any which way he pleases, even in his grandmother's nightgown for all I care. Frankly, I couldn't give a tinker's damn." Garth smiled, blinked and shrugged his shoulders and reached for a slice of bread to mop up the gravy on his plate.

Hawks would have been more of a problem! I'd need him here like a bag of hammers.

Just then Dennis walked into the room. He took a seat at the table and commenced to load his plate. He was short, thickset, and built like a bull dog.

Before introducing himself, Garth thought, *He might just be a swell fella despite his looks.* They shook hands.

"Looks. like we are partnered up for the next call," said Garth.

"I guess so," he replied, in a deep voice void of interest, then helped himself to more food that was being passed his way.

***

Fire Station No. 5 had been experiencing a lull in activity for a few days. There were no fires, other emergencies or calls to help out in other districts, but as the men were well aware, things could change in an instant.

It was two o'clock in the morning when the call came in:

"Residence fire at corner of 6TH and Bruce Street!"

Garth leapt out of bed, stepped into his bunker suit and headed out the door. The fire engine was ready as the door was raised so Garth jumped in. The driver came running and was handed the address from the man in the Watch Box. But where was Dennis? Responding to an emergency with immediate effect, Garth had failed to notice where Dennis was at this time.

"Looks like Dennis is missing," said Garth. "Go ahead without us, I'll check on him and we'll catch up . . . we're wasting precious time talking, so hurry."

He jumped out, slammed the door shut and then they drove off. He ran back to the dorm. Halfway there he could hear a man hollering in agony. When he entered the room, he could see Dennis sitting on the edge of his bunk, naked as a jay bird and moaning. Tears were running down his face.

"Dennis, what on earth's the matter?"

"I'm stuck, I'm stuck"" he called out.

Garth was trying to quickly access the situation but could not figure out what the problem was.

"Are you afraid to go out on a call?" was the best he could muster.

"Hell no, man, I cannot move. Goddamn it!"

Garth examined closer and could not believe his eyes.

The poor bugger! If this ever gets out, he'll be the top joke of the fire hall for years to come.

Dennis had swung his legs out of bed and placed his feet on the floor, and in doing so, the mattress had slid back exposing and spreading the springs just enough for his testicles to fall in. When he removed his weight by trying to stand up, the spring closed again, pinching and clasping his testicles like a vice.

"Oh shit! You poor son-of-a-gun! I don't want you to move. I'm going to slide under the bed and spread the springs as best I can to release them. I will holler for you to stand up."

"OK," he panted, "I won't move."

Beads of perspiration had formed on his forehead.

Garth slid under the low bed that, like the rest in the dorm, was donated by the Army Corp. He could see the ridged appendage hanging—veins bulging and turning blue. He grabbed the spring on either side trying not to pinch the genitalia. The springs were strong and seemingly immovable. Garth did not have room for the leverage needed. Finally, mustering brute force in both arms, he grunted and finally managed to spread the springs on either side. He called out in a long course whisper, "Stand up!"

Dennis did so and then reached down to see if he had missing body parts; it felt like they'd been pinched off.

Success!

All body parts were intact.

"What a relief!" exclaimed Dennis. "Thank you—uh, please, please don't tell anyone about this. Ya know what'll happen if the guys get wind."

"No one will hear it from me." He glanced down and continued, "But I do believe, because of their colour, I should take you to the hospital to be checked over. I'll drop you off and head over to the fire. It'll probably be out by the time I get there. No doubt you'll have a long wait in the emergency. I'll be around to pick you up later."

"What will I tell them happened?"

"I'm sure you can think of something other than the truth."

"If the boys ask why I didn't respond to the alarm, what will you tell them?"

Garth thought for a moment, scratched his head and said, "That's easy, you sprained your ankle getting out of bed."

Dennis nodded with a thankful look on his face but Garth could see he was still in pain.

"One more thing, Dennis. From now on wear pyjamas. Damn it!"

With his legs parted like a toddling child, Dennis followed Garth for the trip to the hospital.

The next day when the men arrived on shift, two men came in laughing and couldn't wait to share their mirth.

"You'll never believe this one. Dennis Jones got his balls caught in the bed spring during the night."

Uproarious laughter erupted.

"Ouch!"

"You gotta be kidding! The poor bugger!"

"How do you know? Maybe it's just a rumour?"

"Hell no, I saw it with my own eyes. I saw someone's feet sticking out from under the bed. Apparently he was trying to free them, don't know who it was, didn't stick around to find out. I had to run. It doesn't pay to sleep in the raw."

The laughter and groans continued for several minutes during the meal.

Garth sat silently thinking, *Cockroach!*

Bob had prepared another wonderful dinner. This time it was Chinese food; once again done to perfection. They sat enjoying their food and discussing the previous night's fire, one that had been quickly extinguished.

Dennis was the last one to come into the kitchen.

He came waddling in like a wounded soldier. When the men saw him, they began laughing again. Several stood up and grabbed their own crotches. Someone shouted, "Gotta take better care of the family jewels, Dennis!"

Dennis knew he was going to have to endure the teasing for days to come. He glanced over at Garth with an accusatory look on his face. Garth shrugged his shoulders, showed his palms as if to say, *I don't know how they found out, wasn't me.*

The razzing continued unmercifully for days and one firefighter, to express the extreme, came into the lunch room with a large bandage wrapped around a baseball hanging down the front of his trousers. There would have to be something of greater significance to put an end to the razzing.

Garth knew that their constant grabbing at humour was merely a catalyst against the gravity of their jobs. He recalled the conversation with Kyla when they were together last evening putting some of the final touches to their October wedding. She had put it most succinctly, "I'm so proud of you, Garth," she had said. "I'm proud of what you do. How brave you are. How you are constantly helping others. No other service industry, can match the challenges you face each and every time you answer a call. Every time I hear a siren, I think of you and pray you'll survive. That's how I feel, honey."

Now, with the mild weather upon them, the trips out to the farm were frequent. Plans for their new home had taken root, footings for the foundation were in place and soon the framing would commence. Days off from the fire station were spent with Kyla riding and working on their new home, while other days were on the job making a living and serving the public. He was happy to know his future wife was proud of his chosen field.

CHAPTER

22

SUNDAY MORNING AND GARTH WAS WORKING THE dayshift. The station was busy with quiet activity. Some of the men were playing pool, others sat chatting at the table with a coffee cup in their hand while others cleaned the floors.

Suddenly, an emergency call came in:

"Number 5 and 18 apartment fire at 83 Maple Street!

Number 5 and 18 apartment fire at 83 Maple Street!"

Closely followed by his colleagues, Garth scurried across the floor. In less than a minute they were ready for action.

As they reached the heavier city traffic, cars wouldn't give them a clear path. They blasted the horn time and time again swinging from one side of the road to the other, sometimes closely avoiding an accident.

At last, they saw the apartment ahead with dark smoke pouring out the middle windows.

Meanwhile, Incident Commander, Chief Watson, was last to leave and to close up the station. He was speeding towards the fire, which now had come into his view. He grabbed his radio, his voice heavy with urgency. "Incident Commander to Fire Chief, we have a working fire. Smoke issuing from windows on about the twentieth floor. Initiate third alarm."

He sped to the scene, took control of the command centre and his broadcast continued: "All units engage high rise procedures.

"Pump 5—assume attack on 19th floor.

"Rescue 5—assume search on 19th floor.

"Pump 18—assume attack on 19th floor."

Chief Wilson planned to allocate likewise procedures to Station No. 3 and requested they report to him immediately upon arrival. He caught his breath and thought, *This is a massive fire! Yessiree!*

Garth and crew had reached their destination and slammed on the breaks. Their earlier vision from the pump now became a reality. The street was cloaked in smoke and the choking smell of a variety of burning material filled the air. Smoke was pouring out some of the windows on the 19th floor; the fire was out of control.

Standing on the periphery was an assemblage of frightened people, most of whom were obviously tenants. Some were crying and clutching a photograph album while others huddled together in shock.

Ambulances and police cars simultaneously pulled up to the curb. A helicopter was circling overhead. From the air, it looked like a disaster zone. A blue and white media truck arrived on scene and commenced filming. Everything was happening so quickly and the smoke kept billowing with intermittent wisps of flames.

More firefighters arrived by bus, and others with self-contained breathing apparatuses ready for use were hurrying with landlines to the 19th floor to converge and push smoke and heat out of the centre apartments and out of area windows. Some were on search and rescue. They entered the building and were hit with smoke growing heavier by the minute. The acrid, choking odour that consumed the air, defied description.

Garth and his partner entered just ahead of others on the search and rescue mission. They took the elevator up to the 18th floor and got out, and then ran the stairs to the 19th floor, which was black with smoke.

They broke down the door of the first apartment and checked each room calling out, "This is the fire department! Anybody here? Hello! Hello!"

Garth quickly opened the windows to allow the smoke to escape and caught a glimpse of other firefighters arriving on scene, including those who had journeyed by bus. Garth and his partner continued their search of the apartment and once satisfied that their search was complete, they chalked the door with a large X and moved to the next apartment.

Throughout each floor of the twenty-six-floor apartment, the effort continued tirelessly in the quest to save lives, find the source of the fire and extinguish it. The size of the building had dictated the call of all the firefighters in the city of Papillon. Personnel with specific equipment had come to help, even the men who were relieved that morning at 8:00 AM had reported to their home station then waited for bus transportation to the fire scene.

When Garth and his partner approached the next door, it was unlocked. They entered the room and through the smoke they could see something or someone on a chair by the window. It was an elderly lady sitting and staring out the window, holding a blanket over her head and coughing. She wasn't alarmed to see firefighters walk into her apartment, which surprised Garth.

It's as though she was expecting us, he thought.

Between coughs she asked: "Why are there so many people outside?"

"There is a fire in this building, ma'am. We have to take you out to safety right now."

"Oh, gracious me!" she declared. "Oh, gracious me!"

Garth spoke in a tender voice: "We will help you. Don't be afraid. Just grab our arms. We'll support you." They helped her out to the hallway, down the elevator and out to a waiting ambulance.

By this time the crowd had become much larger; so many people just wanted to see what was happening. They came from all corners of Papillon. Some had lawn chairs as if it were a picture show and others were just standing there waiting to see some flames. In an otherwise quiet part of the world, this was considered to be a big event.

Garth and his partner hurried back in and continued their search. The next three apartments were empty. They continued their search: door by door, room by room, closet by closet, under beds, behind doors and furniture, behind the shower curtain in bathtubs. Always they shouted out, "Hello, hello, anybody here? It's the fire department!"

Two landlines from each end of the high-rise were converging to push smoke and heat out the windows of all the apartments. And right on their heels were two attack firefighters with landlines ready to use if needed.

The smoke was thickening within the odorous hallways. Garth and his partner came to apartment 1911, the last apartment on the 19th floor. Garth stopped short. He could see excessive smoke pouring out from beneath the door. He placed his hand on the door and it was hot. He beckoned to the attack crew to get ready.

"Stand back, I'm going to kick the door in."

It took two kicks to open the door. The men jumped back as flames shot out and the attack crew raised their lines and sprayed. The flames died down somewhat and steam poured forth. When it abated the firefighters could see it obviously was a meth lab—a meth lab gone terribly wrong.

The apartment had been converted into a large room. It housed pressure vessels, reaction chambers and buckets of volatile and dangerous solvents and acids.

They conducted a quick search and ascertained there were no people in the lab.

The fire attack crews were gaining control when suddenly there was a large blast exploding the walls and blowing debris out the windows and down onto the crowd below, who screamed and ran off in different directions.

"Men down! Men down! Men down!" rang out over the radio!

There were two crews of four men each at the staging area with breathing apparatus ready to go. They had heard the cry and raced up the stairway to the 19th floor to rescue the firefighters that were on attack at the blast scene. Rescue became primary and fire attack secondary. All of the firefighters were rescued, or so they thought.

Crews were allocated to the 20th floor to ventilate and attack the fire issuing from the ceiling that had blown up from apartment 1911.

Back at the staging area, the captain shouted in a panic-stricken voice, "Where is Garth Winters? Where the hell is Winters? I don't see Winters!"

His voice had become thunderous.

"I was sure he was right behind me," said Garth's partner.

The blast had disorientated the crews who had been working on the 19th floor and had created an ongoing blaze. To go back up there would be treacherous.

"I'm going up to find him," said a firefighter.

"Like hell you are, it's much too dangerous."

But the firefighter was running up the stairs as fast as his legs could carry him and before the captain could stop him.

**

It was 4:25 PM, and almost time for Kyla Jones to finish her day at work. She sat at her desk listing things to do in her diary, when she looked out the window to see smoke several streets over.

I wonder if Garth is involved. He must be. He was working dayshift today.

When she stepped into her car for the drive home, she turned on the radio.

"We interrupt the local programming to bring you the following broadcast:

"Two firefighters are in hospital with undetermined injuries following their gallant effort in helping fight a fire today. The three-alarm fire in the apartment building located at 83 Maple Street, was extinguished a short while ago. It is reported the fire had been restricted to the 19th and 20th floors. There were no fatalities; the firefighters had been successful in evacuating all of the residents. We will have a full report on the six o'clock evening news."

Kyla's heart was racing. *Hopefully Garth wasn't involved,* but she needed to put her worries to rest.

I know I drive right past the hospital on my way home. I can drop in and see if he's been admitted.

With that thought in mind, she pulled out of the driveway and headed to the hospital.

To her dismay, when she entered the hospital there was a long line ahead of her at the inquiry desk. Nurses and doctors were scurrying about. When she heard a doctor being paged to go to the operating room, she wondered if it was for Garth.

I've got to stop this paranoia, think positively.

"Can you tell me if Mr. Winters has been admitted today?" she asked the beleaguered clerk.

The clerk flipped through the wheel of patients on her desk. She stopped at 'W'. "Would that be Garth Winters?" she asked.

"Yes," she said anxiously. "Garth Winters."

Kyla's hunch was right.

"He's on the second floor in Intensive Care. He's only allowed to have family visit."

"I'm his fiancée. What is his room number?" She felt like screaming.

"Room 221."

Kyla bypassed the elevator and ran up the stairs. She was breathless when she reached the second floor, and her heart was pounding as she approached his room. She looked through the window of the door before opening it.

Garth lay in his bed hooked up to tubes in his nose and his wrist. He had an oxygen mask over his mouth. She could see his face was encircled red, obviously a burn where the breathing apparatus did not cover.

Her hands flew to her cheeks in horror.

My poor, darling man!

She walked slowly towards his bed. When he saw her, he winked. She buried her face on his chest and stifled a sob. He managed to move his one free arm enough to stroke her elbow. Garth wished he could talk to her—wished his mouth wasn't covered so he could comfort her and tell her he was going to be alright.

They stayed like that for some time until Kyla felt another presence in the room, causing her to stand up. The young man that stood before her was obviously a doctor. He wore a white jacket and a stethoscope.

"I'm Doctor Reimer," he said. "Mr. Winters is a very lucky man. He has only minor lung damage and will be released in twenty-four hours. I'll be keeping him on oxygen until he goes home and then I want him to rest for a few days. It could have been much worse— much, much worse—if he hadn't been rescued when he was."

"I'm his fiancée," said Kyla. "We are getting married in a couple of months. I can't tell you how happy I am to hear he'll be alright. I've been so, so worried!" She dabbed her eyes and Garth squeezed her hand.

The next day Chief Watson paid a visit to Garth. He wore a big smile as he walked into the room.

"How are you doing, big guy? They told me at the desk you will be leaving this afternoon after the doctor comes in and signs your discharge."

"I'm having a little trouble breathing, however, other than that, I'm just fine. Wow, the doctor told me I'm lucky to have been rescued. How is the other firefighter who came in the same time I did?"

"I've heard he will be fine too. He has some burns on his hands but nothing serious. He's one brave man!"

"Before I leave today, I want to pay him a visit and thank him. I owe him my life."

"He's on the next floor, Room 331," said the chief. "I'm on my way. We'll see you back at work when you're feeling well again."

As the chief was walking out, Kyla was walking in to give Garth a ride home.

"Hi, sweetheart, do you mind waiting in the lobby for a few minutes. I want to go up to the next floor and thank the firefighter who saved my life."

Kyla nodded and smiled, "But of course, dear!"

He rode the elevator up one floor and walked slowly down the hall looking for Room 331. When he located the room, he walked in and could see the back of a patient sitting in a wheelchair, looking out of the window. As he approached the patient, he could see his hands were bandaged with only the tips of his fingers exposed. There was a strong smell of antiseptic in the room.

"I've come to thank you," said Garth.

Without turning to face him, the man said, "Just doing my job," in a raspy tone.

"You did much more—you saved my life and got burned in the process. How are your hands?"

"They're healing."

There was a small edge of familiarity to the voice. Garth was wondering if he knew him. He wished he would turn around.

"How are *you* doing?" the man asked breaking the awkward silence.

"I'm fine. I'm going home today—need to rest for a few days. Please turn around and let me see your face."

Again there was awkward silence. The noise of the hospital took over: nurses talking in the hallway, a voice paging over the PA system, cleaning staff bumping along doing their work, and in the distance, the familiar sound of a siren could be heard.

Garth waited patiently with many thoughts tripping across his mind. He thought about all that happens behind the smoke.

At last, the motorized chair spun round and Garth gasped when he saw the man that had saved his life.

It was Marvin Hawks.

Marvin looked at him and said, "Don't hit me."

Garth laughed sheepishly. He wanted to shake his hand but couldn't because of the bandages. The most he could do was pat his shoulder. A thought came to his mind.

"I'm getting married in October. Will you be my Best Man?"

Marvin was speechless and his eyes were wide with surprise. All he could do was smile and nod his head in agreement.

A friendship born through gratitude and forgiveness is life's most beautiful!

THE END

GLOSSARY

Aerial: Fire truck with ladder

Apparatus: All equipment used in fighting a fire.

Pump: Regular fire truck.

Resuscitation: Performing artificial respiration.

SCBA: Self-Contained Breathing
                     Apparatus—(Oxygen Mask).

Stringing a line: Taking a water hose to point of fire.

Ferragene .